"Please, Rucker." Dinah abruptly slid to the floor in front of him and repeated raggedly, "Please."

"Don't beg," Rucker said savagely. "You never begged anybody for anything in your life. You're the proudest person I know."

She wrapped both arms around his legs. "I never had to fight like this before. I'll do anything you want."

He couldn't stand it. He bent quickly, grasped her under both arms, and lifted her up. A shudder wracked him as he took her in a tight embrace. She shook just as violently as she burrowed her face into the warm hollow of his neck.

"Hate me if you have to," she murmured brokenly. "Don't trust me. I'll understand and I'll still love you." Her voice grew hoarse with determination. "But help me do what I have to."

"I'm a fool," he muttered. "Because I can't stop wanting to trust you."

"Then do it. Take the chance. . . ."

WHAT ARE *LOVESWEPT* ROMANCES?

They are stories of true romance and touching emotion. We believe those two very important ingredients are constants in our highly sensual and very believable stories in the *LOVESWEPT* line. Our goal is to give you, the reader, stories of consistently high quality that may sometimes make you laugh, sometimes make you cry, but are always fresh and creative and contain many delightful surprises within their pages.

Most romance fans read an enormous number of books. Those they truly love, they keep. Others may be traded with friends and soon forgotten. We hope that each *LOVESWEPT* romance will be a treasure—a "keeper." We will always try to publish

LOVE STORIES YOU'LL NEVER FORGET
BY AUTHORS YOU'LL ALWAYS REMEMBER

The Editors

Katie

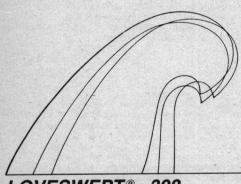

LOVESWEPT® • 308
Deborah Smith
Never Let Go

BANTAM BOOKS
TORONTO • NEW YORK • LONDON • SYDNEY • AUCKLAND

NEVER LET GO

A Bantam Book / February 1989

*LOVESWEPT® and the wave device are registered
trademarks of Bantam Books, a division of
Bantam Doubleday Dell Publishing Group, Inc.
Registered in U.S. Patent
and Trademark Office and elsewhere.*

*If you would be interested in receiving protective vinyl
covers for your Loveswept books, please write to this address
for information:*

Loveswept
Bantam Books
P.O. Box 985
Hicksville, NY 11802

ISBN 0-553-21959-6

Published simultaneously in the United States and Canada

---

*Bantam Books are published by Bantam Books, a division
of Bantam Doubleday Dell Publishing Group, Inc. Its trademark, consisting of the words "Bantam Books" and the
portrayal of a rooster, is Registered in U.S. Patent and
Trademark Office and in other countries. Marca Registrada.
Bantam Books, 666 Fifth Avenue, New York, New York 10103.*

PRINTED IN THE UNITED STATES OF AMERICA

O   0 9 8 7 6 5 4 3 2 1

To Edythe, M.P., and Myra Ann—
three darned good
Alabama Smiths

One

The ocean breeze curled into an open bedroom window and stroked his skin. The afternoon sun was a melting kiss on his naked back. Half-awake, he smiled. The breezes had a seductive appeal that made him think of his wife's touch.

Soft lips brushed his ear. She was the ally of the breeze and the sunshine then. Appropriate, he thought. Her tongue teased his earlobe for a moment. "Every woman needs a man," she whispered huskily. "And you're mine. I think I'll take advantage of that fact."

He growled in mock protest and asked, "Without my permission?"

Her fingers feathered down his belly and explored gently. "It shouldn't be a problem." She dipped her head and placed nibbling kisses along the side of his throat. "You taste like the ocean. Are you sure you're not a merman?"

"Nah. I'm Flipper. Or a giant crab."

She pushed at him gently, guiding him onto his back while she knelt beside him. He kept his eyes shut and inhaled deeply, loving the mingled scents of her light perfume and the ocean air.

"A very fine crab," she told him, as she skimmed her

mouth over his. He smiled to himself and arched into the languid movements of her hands.

"I'm bein' seduced."

"No, I think one has to resist in order to qualify for seduction. You're not resisting at all."

His fingers itched to touch her. He lifted a hand slowly until it contacted with something warm and incredibly smooth. Eventually, after some detouring, he identified that something as the lower part of her stomach. He twisted a finger into the soft curls there.

"You've just lost your last protest against seduction," she informed him, her voice airy. "I believe you're actively participating."

"I admit it. I have no virtue." He sighed dramatically.

She bent over him, cupping his face in her hands. In between soft kisses she murmured, "I'll still respect you in the morning."

"This is my first time, you know."

She nuzzled his head back and kissed the underside of his jaw. Her lips vibrated with suppressed laughter. "Ah, yes. You're thirty-nine years old and still pure. The man *New Southland* magazine once put on a list of the 'Ten Sexiest Writers.' The man Oprah Winfrey called a 'dynamic hunk of cornbread women love to pamper.' "

"I'm . . . I'm really just an innocent country boy at heart," he said plaintively. "And you're a wicked rich girl raised in Atlanta. A debutante. With a high IQ. And a *politician.* Oh, woe is me."

"I'll be very gentle. I'll tell you exactly what to do. Don't worry."

"Should I do this?"

She shuddered with pleasure as his exploring hand slid between her legs. "Y–yes."

"My, that gets a reaction." Her head drooped onto his shoulder when he moved his fingers with wanton skill. He turned his face toward hers and whispered, "That's pretty sexy. What should I do now?"

She nearly whimpered. "Don't stop."

He raised his other hand to one of her breasts and stroked the nipple. His voice became a low rumble. "Creep a little closer, lady crab."

She moaned softly and moved forward so that he could kiss her breasts. Bracing an arm by his head, she nestled her face in his pillow and rocked back and forth.

"I reckon I'm doin' this right?" he asked, his lips against her nipple.

Her soft squeak made him chuckle. He quieted as his own throbbing need made him breathless. His fingers continued to delve into the warm reception between her thighs. "I see that you still like what a rowdy old dirt dauber like me can do to you."

"Not a rowdy old dirt dauber *like* you. Only you. Just you. I love you so much."

He tilted his head back and kissed a spot over her heart. "Love you. Love you forever, ladybug." With a soft groan of pleasure he pulled her over his body, then opened his eyes lazily. The sight of her, her breasts and stomach misted with desire, her face full of devotion, nearly ruined his control. He brushed a fingertip over her hip. "As Spencer Tracy said about Kate Hepburn, 'There's plenty of her, and every ounce is choice.' "

She gave him a gently rebuking look, but smiled. "I believe you've twisted that a bit. He said that there wasn't much of her, but what there was, was choice. I'm nearly *zaftig*—all the fault of adopting your penchant for fried chicken and biscuits."

"*Zaftig*? I thought you were a Libra." He tried to dodge the playful cuff she aimed at his ear and tweeked her breast in retaliation. Her eyes melted with emotion and she squeezed her thighs around him erotically.

"You're not *zaftig*," he assured her. "That's just a polite German word for 'plump.' You're not plump. You're not even German."

She chuckled in delight as he placed both hands on

her hips. Guided by his touch, she sheathed him with silky welcome. Her eyes half-shut and face rosy with desire, she appeared ready to purr with happiness.

"What do I do now, ma'am?" he asked coyly.

"Draw your knees up a little."

"Yes, ma'am." He laughed and circled his hips under her. She gasped and tried to move in sync with him, but he held her still. "Like this, teacher?" he asked.

"Yes. Oh, yes. Yes, my darling."

"You're the only woman in the world who can say 'my darling' without soundin' phony or stuck-up."

"Because I use it sincerely." She stroked his chest with quick, distracted movements, her fingers burrowing into the curly hair. "My darling good old boy."

He shut his eyes tightly and willed his body to slow down. "As much as you need, for as long as you need it," he promised. "I aim to please."

She chuckled sexily. "How gallant." She folded from the waist so that her breasts grazed his chest each time he moved under her. She slid her hands around him and hugged him tightly, resting her head on his shoulder.

He raised a hand and cupped the back of her neck. He kept the other hand on her hips and held her to him that way while she quivered and called his name. Every contraction of her body resonated through him, drawing his own heat closer to the surface until he heard himself whispering inarticulate phrases created of love and release mingled with her name.

A few minutes later, curled against him spoon-style, she fell asleep. He watched her a while, stroking her hair gently. He dozed off and woke eventually to her light kiss. She had moved from beside him.

"Sweetheart, I'm going to run into town. I'll be back in about thirty minutes."

"Hmmm? Why?"

"I'm just going to buy some milk."

"Be careful. Hurry back." He pulled her to him for a jaunty smooch. "Love you."

"Love you too, big guy."

He drifted toward sleep again, but knew that she held his hand for a moment before she whispered good-bye.

She never came back.

Seated at a table in a dingy gallery that overlooked the waiting room of Surador's only airport, Rucker McClure tried to remember the last time he'd felt like laughing.

That was easy—last summer, on vacation. Before Dinah left their Florida vacation house to buy a lousy carton of milk. Before everything good in his life was ripped apart by confusion and grief.

He heard an elderly woman scream an oath in Spanish. People in the crowded room swiveled toward her, and she clasped her hands over her mouth as Suradoran soldiers raised their rifles. She pointed at the fat brown pig who flopped happily in the basket of fruit she'd brought to sell to travelers.

A collective sigh of relief rose in the muggy air as everyone turned back to his or her business. The soldiers, smiling thinly, lowered their guns. The woman put a bare foot against the pig's rump and shoved him hard. He squealed but refused to move. For a moment people forgot their nervousness and chuckled.

"Revolution," the man across from Rucker said. "You can smell it here."

"What part are we secretly playin' in South American politics this time?"

Jeopard Surprise, a master at hiding emotion, simply arched one blond brow and smiled. "We—as in the CIA? I wouldn't know. That's not my game. I work free-lance for Uncle Sam."

Rucker gazed at his friend through slitted eyes. "You know a helluva lot more than you tell me."

Jeopard met his gaze squarely. Rucker's deeper inference had registered. "About some things. Not about Dinah."

"And I don't believe what you've told me about her."

"That's why you're going to see for yourself."

Rucker started to say something else, but Jeopard held up one hand. The tilt of his head told Rucker that he was listening to the tiny transmitter hidden in his ear. Rucker's body tightened. Nerves that had already been tortured and tested too often over the past months now became even more alert.

"She just arrived," Jeopard said. "Diego de Valdivia is with her. There are two others, probably bodyguards."

Rucker vaulted to his feet and swept a gaze over the noisy, colorful throng below. "Where?"

Jeopard stood also. "They're at the checkpoint. But the guards won't dare delay a VIP like Valdivia."

Rucker shoved his chair back. "I'm goin' downstairs."

Jeopard blocked his way. His voice soft but grim, he said, "I know this is putting you through hell, but don't blow it, pal. I've never let a civilian in on something like this before. Valdivia is an agent for the Russians—and the coldest s.o.b. I know, except for myself. Keep that in mind. I'll be listening in case you need some help."

Rucker's voice was lethal. "You mean you'll be recordin' everything so you'll have more reason to arrest Dinah when she gets to the States."

Jeopard nodded slowly. "That, too. We're talking about espionage and treason."

Rucker started to push past him, then halted abruptly. His voice low and vicious, he noted, "*You're* talkin' about espionage and treason. *I'm* tryin' to learn what's happened to somebody I love."

• • •

He found a corner and waited. People stared at him. An old man with the features of a *mestizo*, mixed Spanish and Indian blood, jabbed a walking cane in his direction, then spent nearly a minute studying his cowboy boots, jeans, white polo shirt, and aviator sunglasses. Finally he focused on Rucker's thick auburn hair and mustache. "Yankee," he sneered.

"I live in Alabama, partner," Rucker said, and the man shuffled off, mumbling.

Rucker's eyes hurt from scanning the crowded area, even though being six foot three gave him an advantage. His throat was dry. He found himself silently repeating, *Where is she? Dear God, where is she?*

The crowd parted as if he'd been heard.

The woman he would have died for moved gracefully through the throng of people and farm animals, sidestepping the roughly woven baskets that served as luggage for most travelers.

Her chocolate-colored hair had grown long; now it was a curling mane that ended below her shoulders. A tailored white dress accented her statuesque height. Her rounded figure had become thin, almost too thin. Around her neck hung a thick gold chain that bore a medallion stamped with ancient Inca designs.

Rucker moved forward, though he wasn't aware of any conscious effort. *Don't you never cry, boy,* his father had instructed Rucker during childhood, enforcing the edict with rough words or fists. Truck drivers didn't cry and neither did their sons.

The rule was stupid, Rucker decided later, but by then it was ingrained. He honored it. A man didn't cry unless the woman he loved disappeared and he spent months tormenting himself with images of what might have happened to her.

A man didn't cry—unless that woman turned out to be totally safe now—and looking cool and lovely even in this godforsaken jungle airport. Rucker's eyes burned and he dug his fingernails into his palms.

She was accompanied by a tall, black-haired man whose impeccable white suit matched the elegance of her beautifully tailored white dress. His features were patrician, Rucker noticed just before he saw them stop. Dinah leaned companionably against the man and his arm went around her shoulders.

Shock and fury flooded Rucker. Jeopard had shown him pictures of her traveling with Valdivia, plus other photographs that left no doubt that she worked for the agent. But he hadn't believed it; couldn't believe it.

There had to be an explanation. He'd come to haul her back home and find out what it was.

Rucker jerked his sunglasses off and dropped them on the room's hard concrete floor without caring. He wanted her to look straight into his eyes. Two hulking men in sport shirts and army fatigue pants shadowed her and Valdivia protectively. Rucker was aware when the men spotted him and reached for the pistols holstered on their belts.

Two more steps. Then one. Then he stopped in front of his wife and stood with his legs slightly braced. She was glancing down at her wristwatch.

Then she looked up.

Later, Rucker spent hours replaying that moment and trying to decipher it. Her eyes were a powder blue shade that contrasted starkly with her dark lashes. People had a hard time looking away from those eyes. They were unique, and when emotion filled them, they were unforgettable.

In the first few seconds after they met his, he saw them widen in disbelief. Then they flooded with the poignant distress of conflicting emotions.

"Rucker," she whispered hoarsely, and his name sounded like a wish come true. She might have been dying before this moment.

He exhaled raggedly and reached for her with one hand. Valdivia said something curt to him in Spanish, and one of the bodyguards shoved his hand away.

Spanish was one of many languages Rucker didn't speak, but that didn't hamper his response. Without taking his eyes from the obvious welcome in Dinah's face, he drawled softly to Valdivia, "Get your damned arm off my wife's shoulders before I kill you."

It wasn't exactly the kind of approach Jeopard had coached him to make.

Immediately the bodyguards started forward. The look of transfixed adoration fled from Dinah's eyes. Her face went white and she flung up a hand in command. "No!" They halted and glanced at Valdivia, who nodded his agreement.

Sighing, she rubbed her forehead wearily and gazed at Rucker in a speculative way. "You always could startle me," she muttered. "I'd forgotten how intense you are."

"You weren't startled. You were damned glad to see me," he noted, frowning.

She drew her shoulders back imperiously. Turning to Valdivia, she said in English, "Diego, you'll have to pardon my husband. I've told you so much about his background that you certainly can't blame him for being belligerent and aggressive, can you?"

Valdivia's dark eyes were unfathomable, but he smiled. "So this is the famous American writer? The modern Mark Twain?"

"Famous. Infamous. Whatever." She turned back to Rucker, an expression of grim amusement on her face. "I'm surprised it took you so long to find me."

Rucker was stunned by the stranger who had replaced his wife. He stared at her silently while contrasting emotions warred inside him. Chief among them was a sick feeling of horror; was Jeopard right about her?

He kept his eyes riveted to hers. "After nearly a year, is that all you have to say to me?"

"Surely you recall that I like everything to be neat. I thought you'd be less wounded if I simply disappeared."

Her voice, full of soft southern intonations that were so much more cultured than his backwoods accent, sounded harsh with strain.

"So instead you left me wonderin' if you were hurt, or kidnapped, or dead," Rucker noted.

She inhaled softly. "I'm sorry that you have a vivid imagination."

He grabbed her forearms and struggled not to shake her. The bodyguards reached for their guns. Dinah looked around anxiously. "No! *Por favor.*" She pulled away from him. "If you don't want to cause a worse scene, you'll control yourself."

His hands stayed in the air, clenching into fists. "Where have you been all these months?"

"With this gentleman." She nodded toward Valdivia.

He bowed slightly. "Señor Diego Correles Juan de Valdivia. It's very interesting to meet you, Señor McClure."

Rucker fought to remember the questions Jeopard had given him. He couldn't help phrasing them his own way. Gesturing toward Valdivia's white suit, he demanded, "What the hell are you? Ricardo Montalban's younger brother? South America's version of Tennessee Williams? An extra from *Miami Vice*?"

"Rucker, don't do this!" Dinah interjected. "Diego, I apologize—"

"Your husband's reputation for humor is certainly well earned, *querida.*"

Anger made scarlet dots on her cheeks as she glared at Rucker. "Señor Valdivia is a respected businessman. He owns the largest coffee and banana plantations in this country."

Rucker jerked a thumb toward the tense bodyguards. "Tell these ugly bean pickers to lay off the caffeine."

"You really *beg* for trouble, Señor," Valdivia said lightly.

"No, he just has more pride than sense," Dinah corrected. She laid a hand on Rucker's arm.

His warning came back soft and deadly. "Don't touch me."

She shrugged, her mouth a tight line of control, and placed her hand back on her white eel-skin shoulder bag. "How did you locate me?"

"I hired people who specialize in finding liars."

"I never lied to you. I left before I *had* to lie to you—about my feelings, about our future together."

"Thanks for carin'."

"Señor McClure," Valdivia interjected. "Dinah and I have a flight to catch."

"When I want to hear from you, I'll ask you a question," Rucker told him curtly. "Where are you going?" he asked Dinah.

"That's none of your business."

Rucker's voice was very deep. Now, filled with fury, it was a fierce rumble. "The hell it isn't."

"I want a divorce. Go back to Alabama and take care of the legalities. I don't want any settlement, so it should be easy." His response to her words was a lethal tightening of body and face; eyes that went dark, icy green; primitive reactions rising to the surface.

Her eyes flickered over him with sudden fear. "If you try to drag me out of here, you'll be killed."

"Undoubtedly," Valdivia added in a pleasant tone.

Rucker wasn't certain that he cared. He held Dinah's gaze, losing his past and future in their cold, unwavering stare.

"There were things you left behind other than me," he finally told her. "Things you loved. Your mother's jewelry. Your trophies."

"Trophies?" Valdivia inquired.

Dinah blinked as if coming back to life and glanced away from Rucker. "Beauty contest trophies," she said.

"She was Miss Gum Spirits of 1973," Rucker noted in a biting tone. He paused, hating himself for this pettiness, hating Valdivia, and wishing he could hate Dinah. "She was Miss Georgia later on, and she could have been Miss America, but she backed out. Something about her personal scruples. Hell, it's too bad she can't give it a second try. Now she has no scruples."

One of her hands lurched out toward him, wavering as if she were desperately looking for support. He was so shocked that he didn't stop to think, he simply held his hand out in return.

"Stop, stop," she murmured, then turned swiftly and grasped Valdivia's arm. "We need to leave, Diego."

"Yes, of course."

"Where did you meet him?" Rucker demanded, nodding toward Valdivia. "Just tell me that."

"Two years ago, when I went to the Conference of the Americas, in New Orleans."

"I had an interest in the political systems of small towns in your country," Valdivia added with a predatory show of teeth that could have been mistaken for a smile. "Dinah, as mayor of that village—what was the name, *querida*?"

"Mount Pleasant."

"Yes. She fascinated me. Step out of the way, Señor McClure."

"Give me an address," Rucker told her. "So I can have my lawyer contact you."

She shook her head. "I have *your* address. Assuming that you still live in Mount Pleasant."

"Yes." *It's my home,* he added silently, *and your home.*

"I'll send you something—whatever the court needs —that absolves you from a divorce settlement."

"Step back, Señor," Valdivia said. The unpleasant edge in his voice caused the bodyguards to inch closer.

"Please," Dinah added. Her eyes begged Rucker. "It's over. I couldn't take anymore. We're too different. We always were. Now go home and forget about me."

A long, harsh breath shattered inside his lungs. "You hid those feeling's well," he said gruffly. "You'd make a great actress . . . or a great prostitute."

"Step back," Valdivia said one more time. "People have a way of walking into the jungle here and never returning. I would hate for you to have such a fate, Señor."

Rucker snatched the man's pristine white lapels into his fist. "Don't threaten me—"

"Stop it!" Dinah interjected. She pried Rucker's fingers off her companion's coat. "Get away from us, Rucker. Leave me alone. Do I have to put it cruelly? All right. You were an embarrassing redneck, but I stayed with you because I had a certain amount of prestige as the wife of a well-known writer—even if all you write are simpleminded books of southern humor."

She continued rapidly, her voice rising. "I left without a word because I was pregnant—and I knew that if you found out you'd never let me go."

Rucker stared at her with horror. "We have a baby and you didn't tell me?"

"There's no baby. I . . . fixed the problem."

Her words numbed him and left nothing—not anger, not shock, not grief. He was dying. It might be years before he stopped breathing, but he could feel himself dying now.

"I came here to find out what happened to you," he said finally. "To see if you were really alive." He paused. When had everything gotten so quiet, and so cold? Or was it just the emptiness growing inside him? "Now I'm not sure you ever existed."

"As far as you're concerned, I didn't."

She stared straight ahead, no longer acknowledging his presence. The bodyguards blocked him as Valdivia guided her past. Rucker's gaze followed her until she disappeared in the crowd, and then he remained still, staring at nothing, aware of nothing until Jeopard's sympathetic grip on his arm forced him to walk away.

March had been steamy in Surador, but here in Ala-

bama, wintertime had not yielded to spring and driz-
zling rain accompanied near-freezing temperatures.
Dinah shivered by the window of her Montgomery hotel room. The night absorbed her with its bleakness.
She quickly pulled the curtains closed, then, moving
woodenly, began to strip off her clothes.

Why had Valdivia detoured to this small southern
city? They'd arrived a week ago; the mission was barely
begun, and she had hoped to be headed back to Surador
by now. Who were they hiding from?

She thought he enjoyed torturing her this way, keeping her within a few hours' drive of her old life, her old
home, and the husband she had so nearly destroyed.

Dinah stepped into a hot shower and leaned against
the tiled wall, her shoulders hunched and her face
buried in her hands. She sobbed loudly, glad for the
freedom to let anguish draw hard shudders through
her body. She could only cry like this in the shower;
Valdivia's room was next door, and the walls were thin.
Any hint of weakness on her part only strengthened
his position.

Here in the shower she could call Rucker's name and
say that she loved him. Here she could promise that
everything would be all right someday. Here she could
grieve over the devastation she'd seen in his eyes.

After nearly an hour she forced herself to leave the
shower's private haven. Valdivia would be coming by
with dinner soon. Probably more hamburgers. His crav-
ing for American junk food would have been funny,
under different circumstances.

Dinah wrapped her dark hair in a towel. She reluctantly donned a lacy black robe and black bedroom
shoes that resembled ballet slippers. Valdivia chose all
her clothes, so there was nothing else to wear. This
sexy outfit was one more way in which he tested her
resistance to intimacy. He was unwilling to force her
because he sensed that it would make her less coopera-
tive.

And as long as he needed her cooperation, she had a chance.

She was startled by the sound of running feet in the hallway outside. Dinah jumped when someone slammed against her door. A heavy fist pounded it.

"Let me in!" Valdivia ordered.

He kept a key to her room and didn't have to ask for admittance. Dinah looked quickly for something to cover her flimsy robe. "Just a second—"

"Immediately, damn you!"

Dinah jerked the door open and hugged her arms over her chest. She staggered back, gasping, as Valdivia hurled himself into the room and banged the door shut.

He was disheveled and panting. His heavy cashmere overcoat hung open, revealing a conservative gray suit with pinstripes. Dinah's gaze went to the red stain widening on the top of one thigh.

Valdivia sank to the bed, his face so ashen that his slender black brows seemed unnatural. "I've been discovered," he rasped in Spanish. "You have to go on alone."

"But—"

"There's no time! They may find us at any moment! I'll have to distract them while you complete our job." He lurched to his feet, staggered to the sliding glass door that opened onto a balcony, and slid it open. "Get your coat!" Stunned, she didn't move. He swung about and stabbed a finger at her viciously. "If you don't do this, you know what will happen! Do you understand?"

Dinah ran for the closet and snatched a coat off a hanger. Swinging the coat over her shoulders, she went to the balcony. Valdivia stood there, surveying the rain-soaked bushes one floor below. They both heard running footsteps far down the hotel corridor.

"I need money, credit cards, *something*," she protested, as he grabbed her wrist and urged her over the balcony railing.

Cursing, he reached into a coat pocket and retrieved a wad of American money, which he thrust into her hand. "Either I or someone else will meet you in New Orleans five days from now. The usual place."

"What if I'm caught?"

He grabbed the front of her coat. Dinah clung to the railing, feeling the towel slide off her head. Icy rain began to pepper her scalp. Valdivia's handsome face was twisted with cruelty.

"*Then you lose everything you love,*" he warned. "Do not fail. And do not tell anyone anything about your situation, unless you want to be responsible for their safety."

Dinah drew back one hand and slapped him, hard. A year ago she would have been incapable of striking another human being. She'd learned to fight. "Keep your part of the bargain, Diego, and I'll keep mine."

With a muffled laugh, Valdivia shoved her off the balcony.

"Lady, did you have a quarrel with your boyfriend?"

Dinah wrapped herself tighter inside the thick sable coat and, for once, blessed Valdivia's penchant for giving her expensive gifts. She huddled in the cab's backseat and tried to keep her teeth from chattering. Her legs stung badly where the bushes had scraped them. One hip ached from the fall.

"Yes. A q–quarrel," she told the driver.

"When I saw you on the sidewalk outside that cheap hotel, I could tell you were desperate to get away. Did he hit you?"

"He wouldn't d–dare."

"Good. What's wrong with him?"

It would take a textbook on sadistic personalities to answer that one, Dinah thought. "He's jealous."

"Where to, now?"

Dinah took several deep breaths and considered that

question for the first time. "Just . . . take the interstate and head north. I have to think."

Her destination was the mountains of eastern Kentucky, at least a nine-hour drive. Dinah rapidly unfolded the wet, crumpled bills in her fist. He'd given her fifty-four dollars.

She almost groaned out loud. Only fifty-four dollars. No credit cards, no ID, no checks, and no clothes, she added grimly. She had learned to live with fear, but not with defeat. Now she leaned her head against the cab's seat and shut her eyes wearily.

Think, think, she told herself. When she did, shivers ran through her, this time from anxiety. She spent several minutes trying to find options, but couldn't. "Do you think a bus ticket to Mount Pleasant would cost less than fifty-four dollars?" she asked raggedly.

The cab driver chuckled. "Where is that?"

"North Alabama. In the mountains near the Tennessee line."

"Yeah, you can get there. Whew! When you run from a man, you run a long way."

Dinah winced. She wasn't running *from* a man. She was running *to* one, the only one who could help her—but the one with the least reason to care.

Two

Rucker slammed his Land Rover into park by the small clapboard house he and Dinah had shared. All evening he'd been driving the mountain roads, just driving, wishing he could think of someplace to go and a reason for wanting to go there.

The darkness of the cloudy March night surrounded him as soon as he turned the headlights off. He put his head back on the truck seat, shoved the door open, and listened to the pine forest rustle in the wind. Rain pattered softly on the truck's roof. The night smelled wet, cold, and lonely.

He hadn't slept in the house since his return from Surador a few days ago. He knew abruptly that he couldn't sleep in it tonight, either. It had been Dinah's home before they married; he'd sold his sprawling house in Birmingham and moved up here. Everything about the remodeled farmhouse spoke of her warmth and class.

It was all a lie.

He gritted his teeth as he climbed out of the Land Rover and pulled the collar up on his aviator's jacket. He'd get a change of clothes and go back to the motel.

He kept wondering when Jeopard's agents would locate Dinah and Valdivia.

His booted feet made hollow sounds on the porch's wide-plank floor. He swung the screen door open, unlocked the main door, reached inside, and flicked on the porch light.

"R–Rucker."

He whirled toward the unmistakable voice. Dinah sat on the floor by a window. Her teeth chattered and her wet hair clung to the collar of a black fur coat that cascaded around her like a luxurious tent. One hand grasped the window ledge. She looked frail and exhausted.

After a stunned moment, Rucker drew a pained breath and forced himself to recall the razor-sharp words she'd spoken to him in Surador. He moved slowly across the porch, then dropped to his boot heels in front of her.

"Lose your Latin meal ticket?" he asked bitterly.

"Yes. I need your help."

Disgust crept into his expression. He ducked his head and rammed a hand through his hair. "Lady, you've got a helluva lot of gall."

"I know." All that mattered was that she was home, where she had dreamed of being for so long, and that she loved him dearly, regardless of what he might do or say because she'd hurt him.

Dinah gazed hungrily at him—at the wavy auburn hair that feathered upward at the ends now that he'd ruffled it, at the width of his shoulders and at the way the faded jeans stretched over his long, powerful legs. She closed her eyes and cherished his scent—the leather of his jacket, traces of rich cigar smoke, the smell of masculine hair and skin.

His deep voice broke her reverie. "Where's Surador's poster boy for sewage control?"

"I don't know." That was true. She licked her chapped lips and his eyes went to the movement. He cursed viciously and looked away.

"Don't jerk me around. What happened to him?"

Fear for Rucker's safety made her very cautious. She pretended to study the sable coat pooled around her on the porch floor and said stubbornly, "You don't need to know. Look, I can't get up. My feet are n—numb. The bus station is two miles from h—here, and I didn't have any money left for cab fare. So I walked."

"What were you doin' broke and on a bus? Did good old Diego lose all his dough? Did the banana market go rotten?"

"I'm on my own now. That's all I can tell you."

Rucker's face was rugged. The dimples of his younger years had become creases on either side of his mouth. Stress and weight loss had deepened them in the months since she left him, giving his face an aged, angular harshness that tore at her heart. It was still, however, the kind of masculine face that hypnotized women. Dinah studied every nuance of his expression, aching to caress the sadness out of it.

"So what do you want from me?"

"I need . . ." Dinah bent her head forward as bright pinpoints of light danced in front of her eyes.

"What? I thought you didn't need anything from me."

She hadn't eaten all day, she'd spent the past hour walking nearly barefoot in freezing temperatures, and her nerves were shot. But she'd learned to hide physical and emotional discomfort so well over the past months that it was a habit now.

"I just need some money," she finally managed. "I have to go somewhere."

"Where?"

"Can't tell you."

Frustration made his voice a hoarse whisper. "Then you can get the hell off my porch."

He stood up. Dinah tilted her head back. A wave of dizziness swept over her and she gripped the window ledge harder, shutting her eyes.

"Are you sick?" he asked, and she nearly cried at his

undertone of concern. All the love was still there. She hadn't lost him entirely.

"N—no. Just cold." She opened her eyes and found him gazing at the sable coat with disgust.

"You can't be cold inside that thing. A present from Valdivia?"

She didn't give an answer because the look on his face showed that he knew the answer. Rucker pivoted on one heel and walked to the front door, his back rigid. "You can have twenty-five bucks. I'll call a cab and you can go back to the bus station. I suggest you head for Birmingham and pawn that coat. Get your butt up and come inside."

How could she pawn the coat when she was wearing only a sheer robe underneath? Besides, if she tried to, she'd raise suspicion. A pawnbroker might call the police.

Dinah stared after him wretchedly. And she couldn't bear to go inside their house. The memories would wreck her. They had made love the first time in this house. "I'll wait out here," she told him.

Rucker kicked the front door open, then turned and stared at her. "Can't take the guilt?"

"We'll both be happier if I just stay here." Her throat tightened. "Rucker, I know you don't have any reason to help m—me, but please. It's urgent. Just a few hundred dollars."

"I wasted a lot of money lookin' for you in the past months. I haven't written a column or worked on a book since you sashayed out the door of that damned beach house in Florida. If you think that I'm gonna toss good money after bad now, you've spent too many days in the hot jungle sun."

"It's a matter of life and death!"

"Whose? Yours?"

"N—no."

"Then I don't give a damn."

His brutality didn't wound her; it was an appropriate

reaction, considering the situation. The man she remembered could be stubborn and macho and domi-
neering, but never cruel. He believed in simple values
but he was an intellectual in his own way, and a phi-
losopher. No heart was more generous or kind.

She couldn't stand to hurt him anymore. She'd do
whatever she had to do to get the money elsewhere.
Her shoulders slumped. "All right," Dinah murmured.
"Just call a cab for me."

She twisted around so that her back was to him,
then reached inside the coat with one hand and rubbed
her cold, stinging feet. The ballet slippers had lasted
for less than a mile, then became more of a hindrance
than a help. Pain spiraled up her legs. The muscles
contracted in her back. She could feel him assessing
her.

"You can either keep secrets from me or you can tell
me the truth and maybe I'll help you," he said abruptly.

"All I can tell you is that I have a job to do, and
there's going to be trouble if I don't do it."

"What kind of job?"

What you don't know can't hurt you, my darling,
she thought desperately. The cliché had never been
more true. If she told him everything he'd undoubtedly
interfere—and Valdivia would undoubtedly have him
killed.

Dinah struggled to keep her voice steady. "Just call a
c—cab before I freeze. There are only two cabs in all of
Twittle County, as I recall. It'll take an hour for one to
get here." Suddenly she couldn't be strong any longer.
Her voice began to break. "Call. Please call. S—stop
looking at me and hating me."

He went inside and slammed the door. Dinah hugged
her head to her knees for a second, then turned fiercely
and grabbed the window ledge with both hands. Enough
self-pity!

She staggered to her feet and leaned against the wall
by the window, wincing at the way her feet ached. She

clutched both arms over her stomach and wished she'd eaten the fast-food egg sandwich Valdivia had brought to her that morning.

The front door banged open and Rucker strode onto the porch again, carrying a heavy quilt. She recognized it as one his mother had made by hand. "Here." He thrust it at her, his eyes trailing down to her newly uncovered feet.

"What the hell?" He threw the blanket onto a chair. "Why are you barefoot in weather like this?"

She swayed a little as fatigue washed over her. "I'm practicing to be an Eskimo."

Rucker studied her bare legs. "What are you wearin' under that coat?"

"Not much. Eskimo training is very strict."

The grimace around his mouth told her that he was imagining how she lost Valdivia and ended up wearing only a sable coat.

"It wasn't that way," she muttered, her eyes burning with despair.

Rucker watched a tiny trickle of blood run down the side of one calf. With a muffled curse, he stepped over to her and jerked the hem of the coat up. The color left his face. "What did he do to you?"

"Nothing. I fell in some bushes. Training for life on the tundra . . ."

"Put a lid on the back talk." Rucker looked at her shrewdly from under thick, expressive brows. "Who was chasin' you?"

She swallowed hard and obstinately shook her head. "Call the cab."

"I think I'll call the police."

Dinah stared at him in horror. The world became fuzzy and unbalanced; her legs collapsed and she realized that she was falling.

Rucker grabbed her, bent forward, and draped her over his shoulder. Dinah gratefully pressed her face against the cool, damp leather of his jacket. When he straightened up blood rushed to her head, clearing it. She chuckled painfully.

"Glad you're enjoyin' yourself," he muttered.

"You're the only man in the world who would toss a fainting woman over his shoulder as if she were a sack of horse feed."

"Yeah, I know my ways don't suit you."

Dinah winced. "I didn't mean it like that."

"You explained how you felt about me already. At the airport."

"I didn't mean it."

He started inside the house. "Then why the hell did you say it?"

Dinah gripped his jacket suddenly. "No! I don't want to go inside!" He clasped the backs of her legs with both big hands. She felt his hold tighten harshly.

"I hope you hate being here. I hope it hurts you the way it hurts me. Now shut up."

Dinah closed her eyes and clung to his jacket as he carried her into the living room. He knelt, let go of her legs, anchored a hand in the back of her coat, and pulled. Abruptly she found herself plopped on a couch.

She opened her eyes reluctantly and looked at the plush, white-on-white furniture and abstract art, the overflowing bookcases, the stone fireplace, and finally, her baby grand piano. A floor lamp cast muted shadows, making the room even cozier than she remembered.

Rucker stood over her, his hands on his hips. She whispered brokenly, "You took good care of everything."

Suddenly she gazed at him with fear. "Where are Jethro and Nureyev?" She had missed the pet possum and talking crow more than she'd ever thought possible.

Rucker's eyes glittered with revenge. "Gone."

"What did you do with them?"

He smiled thinly. With all the traveling he'd done in the past months, there'd been no way to take care of either pet. He'd loaned them to a petting zoo run by the state wildlife commission. Despite the best care, only Jethro had flourished. "Nureyev died. And what I did with Jethro is none of your business."

"Nureyev died?" she asked in a small, hurt voice.

"Yeah. His last words were a quote from your ol' favorite, Sartre. You would have loved it."

Rucker watched grief wash across her eyes. It jumbled his anger and he turned away, his hands clenched. He'd never tell her that he'd taken her cantakerous pet crow to one of the best veterinary specialists in the country, or that he'd sat beside the ailing bird for hours, stroking his head and asking him not to die.

"Will you call the cab now?" she asked, her tone weary.

Rucker swiveled toward her again. "Hell, yes."

He removed his jacket, slung it across a recliner, then strode to a phone on a sleek walnut end table. Dinah curled her toes into the cream-colored carpet and remembered a cold winter afternoon when they'd lain there in front of the fireplace.

Rucker had wrestled her new engagement ring away from her and given it to Nureyev. The crow had swooped around the living room with a four-carat diamond in his beak, perversely happy to be chased by a naked woman. Finally he dropped the ring into Rucker's glass of chocolate milk.

Roaring with laughter, Rucker had invited her to "go fish." She'd emptied the glass on his stomach, then used her tongue to clean him up and retrieve her ring. He hadn't minded the milk bath at all. And Nureyev had talked nonstop from satisfaction over his role in the antics.

"Can't get anybody," Rucker told her, and slammed the phone down.

Dinah wiped her eyes and cleared her throat roughly. She couldn't expect Rucker to believe her sorrow. "Could I have something to eat? Anything—a glass of milk, crackers?"

"Doesn't the banana king feed you?" He studied her

face. "No, I reckon he doesn't. You look like you've lost about twenty pounds."

"You're thinner, too."

"I spent lots of time eatin' at bars. A diet of nothin' but booze and pretzels works like a charm." He went to the kitchen, angrily jerking the cuffs open on his plaid sport shirt. Dinah watched through the open door as he rolled up his sleeves. She got to her feet and shuffled after him, stopping in the doorway.

"Why don't you just drive me to the bus station?"

"I like holdin' you prisoner. It gives me a sense of revenge." He opened a can of soup and dumped it into a small pot on the stove. His knuckles were white from the force of his grip on the pot handle. "So tell me. Is it true what folks say about Latin lovers? Just how big *are* the bananas in Surador?"

Dinah's heart twisted with sorrow for him. "I work for Valdivia. I don't sleep with him."

He made a disbelieving sound and kept his gaze on the pot of soup. But she saw his chest contract as if he were holding his breath. "I know you used to have all sorts of notions about changin' the world. I thought you planned to start in your own country, not some jungle dictatorship."

"I'm never going back into politics."

He chuckled harshly. "Not in this country, at least. But you don't want to waste your nice little *summa cum laude* master's degree in political science." His voice dropped to a fierce rumble. "Hey, this'll be funny to you. The folks here in town just finished settin' up a memorial to their long-lost mayor. A big granite stone. It's in the square right next to the Civil War cannon. The garden club is gonna plant flowers around it. They think you're dead."

Dinah went to a kitchen chair and sank down. She propped her chin on one fist and stared out a bay window into the stark, forbidding night, tears slipping down her cheeks. She had loved being mayor of Mount Pleasant.

She'd planned to run for state representative. Rucker had always declared that she'd be governor one day. That had been her dream until Valdivia stepped into her life.

"You don't believe what I said about Valdivia," she murmured. "That I don't sleep with him."

"Nope. Don't believe anything you tell me."

She stood, wiped her face with the back of one hand, and said calmly, "I love you. I never stopped loving you. I want you to know that, whether you believe it or not."

He froze in place, his jaw working angrily. "You killed our baby."

Dinah shut her eyes and wished she'd had time to make up a less devastating reason for leaving him. He was strangling on the lies she'd told to protect him from Valdivia, and there was nothing she could do about it. She pivoted stiffly and left the room.

"What are you doin' in there?"

"Taking a bubble bath."

Rucker kicked the bathroom door open and she instinctively cringed, covering her chest with crossed arms. The memory of something Valdivia had done was still too clear and she started trembling.

Rucker walked in carrying a bowl of soup and a glass of milk, his face so tense that he could barely talk. "Don't shake like a scared rabbit," he ordered. "I won't touch you."

He set the bowl and glass on the edge of the tub. His eyes scanned her huddled form, nonetheless. Suddenly he reached into the tub and grabbed the ankle nearest to him. Frothy water sloshed over the tub's rim as he jerked her leg up and examined the red scratches that started above her knee.

"That's a helluva tundra you've been runnin' through, Eskimo. I'll see if I've got some antiseptic."

Tenderness welled up inside her. She made a yearning sound in her throat and began to lower her arms. His mouth thinned with control. He released her ankle immediately and stood up.

"We're not gonna trade sex for the money you need."

Dinah cried out sadly. "That wasn't what I—"

But he was already out the door, slamming it behind him.

When she finished drying off she put the fur coat back on and twisted her slinky black robe into a small bundle of silk which she hid in the back of the bathroom linen closet.

Dinah opened the bathroom door and gazed down in astonishment at the neatly folded white jogging suit laying on the floor outside. The sight of the familiar old outfit brought a poignant ache to her chest. Rucker had always loved this outfit on her.

She dropped to her knees and clasped the soft material to her face, inhaling its fresh soap scent, the scent of Sunday afternoon washing.

"Change into that and put the damned coat where I can't see it," Rucker told her.

She looked down the hallway toward the living room. He stood there, legs braced apart, defensive as always. He pointed at the sable. "I don't want to see that ugly pelt again until you leave."

"Okay."

She smiled at him and he frowned. Dinah retreated back into the bathroom, holding the jogging suit to her chest as if it were a good luck charm.

When she walked into the living room a few minutes later, he was sitting on the hearth reading the directions on a tube of ointment. A fire crackled on the grate behind him. He glanced up briefly then commented, "At least your hair looks better."

"Thank you." She curled up on the couch and wondered how she'd ever be able to maintain her casual expression. She couldn't stop watching the sensual play of firelight on him. Red and gold streaks shone in his rumpled hair; flickering shadows highlighted his rough-cut features and thick mustache.

Her lips parted in a sigh while a sweet feeling of desire melted inside her. She felt her body flush as warmth spread up her abdomen and across her breasts. How many nights had she lain alone in the dark, imagining every detail of him, almost feeling his touch?

"Your hair got long," he said brusquely, without looking up.

Dinah hid a smile. He couldn't pretend to read the antiseptic's instructions much longer. "Do you approve?"

"Do you care whether I do or not?"

"Yes." She had vowed not to cut her hair until she returned to him for good. It was a talisman of hope.

"Hmmph. Now that it's all braided, you look more like yourself. Seein' you with messy hair is like seein' the *Mona Lisa* with a frown."

Dinah patted the fat French braid that extended down the middle of her back. "I turned thirty-one last fall. I have a few gray hairs now."

"I have plenty. They're all in my beard, though."

She looked at him sadly. "I've never seen you with a beard."

"I grew one for a while last fall."

Dinah's chest tightened. He had grown the beard soon after she left. "Why? You always disliked beards."

"Shavin' was just too much trouble."

She nodded, understanding the hidden meaning. He hadn't cared how he looked. She had gone through the same phase. "I bet you did a fair imitation of a grizzly bear."

"That's what Millie said. She made me shave it off for her wedding."

Dinah blinked back tears. Millie Surprise had been Rucker's secretary and a good friend to both of them. They had played matchmaker between her and a rowdy country and western singer named Brig McKay. "When did Millie and Brig get married?"

"About six months ago. They're livin' in Nashville."

He didn't mention that just before the wedding Millie and Brig made an unannounced visit to Mount Pleasant, where they found him asleep in the middle of his living room floor, surrounded by beer cans, with Jethro perched on his stomach gnawing a slice of cold pizza. For a few minutes Millie had cried with heartfelt sympathy. Then she went on a rehabilitation rampage.

Dinah hesitated, gauging her words carefully. "I suppose they think I'm dead."

Rucker tossed the tube of ointment to her and stood up tensely. "That's what everybody decided. When there wasn't any ransom note we knew you hadn't been kidnapped. Since your pocketbook was still in the car when the police found it, we knew you hadn't been robbed."

He paused, and she saw tendons flex in his neck. His next words were very low and controlled. "So, the chief theory was that somebody had seen you in town, liked what he saw, so he followed you and ran your car off the road. And then . . ." Rucker stopped and studied her grimly. "You get the drift."

"But you never stopped looking for me." Dinah hugged herself and looked at him in mute agony. "You went through hell," she whispered.

His body stiffened and his chin rose. Dinah realized wretchedly that she'd just reminded him of all his reasons for despising her.

"I called for a cab again, while you were takin' a bath," he said in a lethal voice. "You can't get one until mornin'." He jerked a hand toward the hall that led to the master bedroom. "Go back there and stay. If I see you before mornin' I'll turn you out of my house."

The bed sheets smelled like Rucker. She slept fitfully, and everytime she woke up she took a moment to burrow her face into the pillow that carried the much-loved scent. Depression weighed on her like a dark mantle and thoughts whirled in her mind. If he'd really wanted her out of the house tonight, he'd have driven her to the bus station.

If only she could break through his anger. She could tell him that she hoped to come back to him soon and never leave him again, but he wouldn't believe it. She'd tell him anyway, in the morning.

Dinah woke around two A.M. and dimly heard his voice. She bolted upright in bed, her skin prickling with fear. Rucker was talking to someone.

Praying that she was mistaken, Dinah tiptoed to the bedroom door. She eased it open. The hallway was dark except for light coming from the living room.

The low rumble was definitely Rucker's voice. Her stomach twisted in dread. She slipped into the hallway and padded closer, her ears straining. She stopped just before the living room entrance. Cold perspiration rose on her forehead.

"I don't want to do this," Rucker was saying, his deep voice so leaden that she barely recognized it. "I know. Keep remindin' me that it's for her own good." There was a long pause as he listened. "All right. Eight A.M. And Jeopard? I don't want you to use any damned handcuffs or anything else that'll humiliate her." He cleared his throat roughly. "Right before you get here, I'll tell her that you know about her and Valdivia working for the Russians."

Dinah sagged against the wall as she heard Rucker place the phone back on its cradle. So Rucker knew about Valdivia's work and her participation in it. And he had turned her in.

Anguish made her groan like an animal caught in a trap. Rucker vaulted to his feet as she entered the living room.

"How could you?" she cried hoarsely. "Rucker, you don't know what you've just done!" He looked down at her with a weary, shattered expression as she wound her hands into his shirt front and tried to shake him. He grabbed her wrists but didn't offer much resistance. "You *can't* let me be put in jail! If I don't accomplish what Valdivia sent me to do . . ."

Her voice trailed off as she struggled to make a decision. Dinah cried against his chest for a second. Then she tilted her head back and looked at him desperately. "You and I have a daughter in Surador. *Her safety depends on us.*"

Three

It was a ploy to win his cooperation. It had to be. But a part of his soul came back to life as he scrutinized her tear-streaked face.

"Isn't that amazin'?" he asked tensely. "First you say you got rid of our baby, then you tell me you didn't. Make up your mind, or come up with a better story."

She wound her fingers tighter into his shirt and spoke as calmly as she could. "I had the baby seven months after I left you. She's three months old now."

He shook his head, angry disbelief shimmering in his eyes. "It won't work. You can't lie your way—"

"Her name is Katherine Ann. After our mothers. Katie. You always wanted our first girl to be named that." Her voice shook. "I didn't forget, honey. We've got our Katie." Dinah touched his auburn hair. "She has your coloring. She's so perfect, Rucker. Katie McClure. You can't turn your back on her. You can't."

Breathing hard, he pushed her away. "What stories should I trust, Dinah? The ones you told me in Surador or the ones you're tellin' me now?"

Dinah moaned softly. "I would have told you *anything* in Surador to make you leave me alone before Valdivia's men hurt you."

He laughed without humor, the sound very sad. "I wish I could buy that."

She stepped close to him again and grasped his shoulders fiercely. "You *have* to."

"So my daughter's in Surador. Where?"

"I can't tell you." He cursed wearily and she interrupted. "The less you know, the safer you are! I wouldn't have involved you in this business at all, except that I was desperate. There was no one else. I want to protect you *and* Katie."

"You're sayin' that you left me for a man who'll kill people to get what he wants? You keep workin' for that bastard even though he threatens your own baby? What kind of woman have you turned into?"

"Why I work for Valdivia isn't important right now." She ground out the next words. "How much do you know about him?"

"He's a damned spy for the Russians. He has contacts in the United States. He's a courier for stolen military secrets. *And you work for him.*"

Her face white, she nodded.

He grabbed her head between his hands. "*Why?*"

Dinah swayed with emotion and shut her eyes. "Don't ask me anything else! I'll explain some day. I swear it. For now, all you need to know is that our baby is a pawn in Valdivia's game. He uses anything he can find to hold power over people. If I don't complete this mission and get back to Surador . . ." She choked and couldn't go on.

Rucker's fingers dug into her hair. "What? Tell me!"

"Katie will disappear. Maybe he'll give her to some South American couple to raise. Maybe he won't go to that much trouble." A shudder ran through her. "Rucker, imagine that you can see her, that you're holding her. She smells sweet, milky. It's that baby smell that even puppies and kittens have. She makes solemn faces at you, and she curls her hands around your fingers, and when she looks at you with wonder in her eyes, you know you'll do *anything* to protect her."

"And what has that *anything* included so far?"

He let go of her and watched her face shrewdly. "I do what I'm told to do," Dinah explained in a formal tone. "And I keep waiting for the chance to bring her home to you."

"What's the matter?" he asked dryly. "Don't spies get vacations? Couldn't you wrangle a long weekend and come to visit?"

"It's not that simple."

"And let me guess—you can't tell me why it isn't."

Her eyes were anguished. "That's right."

"Then to hell with your tale about us havin' a daughter. You can't prove it, and I've heard better sob stories from winos beggin' for quarters."

"I can prove it," she countered. Dinah looked down at herself. She wore only the top to her white jogging suit. Because she'd lost weight, it hung to midthigh. With one swift movement she grasped the loose garment, pulled it over her head, and let it fall to the floor.

The silence held the kind of deceptive stillness found at the center of a hurricane. Stunned, Rucker let his eyes flicker down her body.

"Look," she instructed, touching herself lightly. "My breasts weren't this big before, were they? The nipples weren't this dark." She walked to the floor lamp and stood within its circle of light. "See the blue veins just under the skin? They weren't like this before. Come closer and look."

He closed the distance between them and stood within arm's reach, his eyes dark with concentration and his expression still showing astonishment.

Dinah lifted one breast and drew a fingertip along the underside. "My breasts were even larger when I was pregnant. Now that they've shrunk a little, I have some stretch marks. See?"

"No. You look like you could model for *Playboy* tomorrow." He added sardonically, "The 'Girls of the USSR' pictorial."

"Look closer."

His head cocked to one side, he bent forward until his face was only inches from her nipple. "Okay. I see a stretch mark."

"Good."

"And on my stomach, too." She touched a spot just above her dark, curly hair. "There. And there. You can see that my stomach isn't as tight as it used to be."

"That's debatable."

She sighed with dismay. "Touch it."

He reached out and probed just beneath her navel. At his touch the brusque, objective mood changed; she inhaled softly and shut her eyes. "Stop. That's enough."

Rucker drew back quickly, and when she looked up at him she saw by his eyes that the contact had affected him, too. "It's softer," he said in a gruff tone. "But not too soft."

Dinah sat down in the recliner nearby. She began to stroke one of her breasts lightly, running her fingers from the top to the nipple, where she tugged a little. "If this doesn't prove what I've told you, then I'll give up."

His eyes never left her hand's languid journey. He sank to his heels beside the chair. After a minute, several large drops of bluish-white liquid appeared at the end of her nipple.

Dinah's hand shook as she slipped a forefinger under the drops and scooped them onto the tip. Her eyes met Rucker's. "Milk," she whispered. She held out her hand.

He studied the fluid for several seconds. She moved her hand closer. "Taste it."

His expression was somber. He frowned at her hand and she knew that his cynicism was warring with this evidence. Suddenly he leaned forward and took her fingertip between his lips.

His mustache brushed her finger as he drew the

milk away with a soft sucking motion. He sat back, studying her while he touched his tongue to his lips.

His gaze went to her nipple. "Once you get it started, does it keep goin' without any help?"

Dinah glanced down and saw that new milk had appeared on the nipple. "Oh. It sort of . . . leaks. It won't continue unless a baby starts to nurse."

Rucker put one blunt, calloused forefinger on her nipple and caught the new milk. He lifted the finger to his mouth and licked it, his expression so intense that she almost smiled.

"Grade A," he said.

"Naturally pasteurized. Full of vitamins. Already sterilized. Just the right temperature. Stores perfectly in two handy containers. Katie loves it."

At the sound of that name his expression became bleak. He bent his head and ran a hand through his hair. They both sat in silent misery. When he looked up at her, his eyes were stern.

"You had a baby. All right. You were probably sleepin' with Valdivia before you left me, so—"

"I wasn't!"

"There's no reason for me to take your word. Why should I believe that it's my baby or that it's safety depends on you gettin' back to South America?"

Dinah gave him a worried, wistful look. "You'll have to trust me. Isn't it worth the risk?"

After a moment of electric waiting, he said, "I can't trust you."

Dinah groaned and covered her breasts, feeling vulnerable and humiliated. She ducked her head and fiercely squeezed her eyes shut. Tears wouldn't do any good. "Just let me get my coat and leave. Tell Jeopard I climbed out a window in the middle of the night. Give me that much of a chance. Please."

"Jeopard would know what really happened."

"Please." She abruptly slid to the floor in front of him. Dinah bowed her head against his knee and repeated raggedly, "Please."

Rucker caught a strangled sound in his throat and stood up. "Don't beg. You never begged anybody for anything in your life. You're the proudest person I know."

She crept closer and wrapped both arms around his legs. "I never had to fight for our baby's life before. I'll do anything you want."

He couldn't stand it. He bent quickly, grasped her under both arms, and lifted her up. A shudder wracked his body as he took her in a tight embrace. She shook just as violently and burrowed her face into the warm hollow of his neck.

"You love the baby," he murmured hoarsely. "I can believe *that.*"

She could feel the muscles working in his throat as he tried to control his emotions. "Hate me if you have to," she murmured brokenly. "Don't trust me. Hurt me. Use me. I'll understand and I'll still love you." Her voice became hoarse with determination. "But help me do what I have to do to protect our daughter."

"I'm a fool," he finally managed to say. "A damned fool. Because I can't stop wantin' to trust you."

"Then do it. Take the chance."

He stepped away from her, his eyes wary. His hand reached absently for the front of his shirt. Rucker touched the damp spot her milky nipple had left. He shut his eyes as if he were being torn apart inside. Twisting around, he bent and picked up her jogging top, then tossed it to her unceremoniously.

"I can't ignore the possibility that you're tellin' the truth about the baby . . . about Katie . . . at least. That's the naive country boy in me."

Dinah closed her eyes and said a small prayer of thanks. She looked at Rucker with devotion. "That's the man I love," she corrected. "The man who knows deep inside himself that he *can* trust me, and that no other person on the face of the earth will ever love him more than I do."

"No." He said the word viciously. "That man died when his wife deserted him to indulge her mysterious ideals about world politics. And the man who took his place is capable of bein' real cruel if she hurts him again. So just keep your distance."

She would only tell him that she had to go north. She'd have a few hours head start before Jeopard arrived at the house intending to arrest her.

Dinah went into the bedroom and opened several dresser drawers. Her throat ached with love as she noted that Rucker had kept all her things exactly as she'd left them. He stopped in the doorway behind her as she drew out underwear, pullover sweaters, jeans, and a blue woolen muffler with matching gloves.

"How long will your little tea party take?" he asked grimly, as he went to a closet and got two small canvas luggage bags. "Or is that information off limits, too?"

"I won't be in the States very long."

"That's about as definite an answer as I'm gonna get, right?"

She turned and looked at him sorrowfully. "Yes. The less you know, the less you'll have to conceal when Jeopard starts grilling you about my 'escape.' "

Rucker came over to the dresser and opened a drawer on his side. Dinah watched in puzzlement as he removed several pairs of athletic socks from an enormous collection of the same.

"Jeopard won't be a problem," he told her without looking up. "Because I'll be with you."

He blithely opened another drawer and removed T-shirts. Dinah dropped her armload of clothes and grabbed his wrist. "No," she said grimly.

"That's the deal. Take it or leave it."

"Rucker, you *can't*. It would make you an accomplice."

"I don't care. You don't have to tell me anything. I won't ask questions. But I'm not lettin' you out of my sight again."

Dinah made a low sound of frustration. "I was afraid of this! Life isn't a John Wayne movie, and you can't ride roughshod over the villains! These Indians don't fight fair!"

"Injuns never fight fair," he said quaintly. "That's why the Duke had to be so tough."

"I won't do it! I won't let you come with me!"

He straightened slowly, all levity gone. He was six inches taller than she, many pounds heavier, and much more inclined to use physical force if need be. "You don't have any choice."

She studied the determination in his eyes and muttered, "Oh, it is excellent to have a giant's strength; but it is tyrannous to use it like a giant."

One corner of his mouth curved up in jaunty defiance. "I reckon that quote's not from a John Wayne movie."

"Shakespeare."

"Shakespeare never had a wife who could worry the horns off a brass billy goat." He arched a brow at her. "I tied you up once a few years ago when you didn't have sense enough to let me help you. Remember?"

Her face burned. "And I suppose that you're prepared to use that Neanderthal tactic again?"

"In the flash of a gnat's eyelash."

Defeat settled on her visibly. Frowning, she knelt down and gathered the clothes she'd dropped. Rucker gazed at her bent head and struggled not to lay a reassuring hand on the silky brunette hair that fanned across her shoulders.

"We can't take your truck," she said abruptly. Her expression anxious, she went to the bed and began stuffing things in one of the bags. "The first thing Jeopard will do is give the state patrol your tag number." She paused, looking even more troubled. "So Millie's brother has been assigned to the Valdivia case. Jeopard must be special."

"His agents call him the Iceman, untouched by human emotion."

"He and Valdivia are a perfect match, then."

"Wrong. Jeopard's got honor. He works for the guys in the white hats."

"Meaning that Valdivia and I don't, right?" An awkward silence stretched between them. She felt Rucker watching her, and she sensed the anger and disappointment that lay beneath his control.

"Right."

"Then you shouldn't get involved with us."

"I got involved the day you promised to spend the rest of your life with me. It's too late to back out now."

Dinah sighed raggedly and changed the subject. "We can't take your truck," she repeated.

"I've already got that worked out."

"How?"

"*My* secret." He tossed his clothes on the bed. "Pack my bag."

She curtsied low. "Yes, your highness."

He almost smiled as he left the room.

Dinah had just finished dressing in running shoes, jeans, and a bulky white sweater when he came back. She turned around and stared at the shotgun he held in the crook of one arm. Startled, she tried to joke.

"I hate to tell you this, Rucker, but we spies don't use James Bond tactics very often. The gun's not necessary."

"Indulge me. It's a symbol of my manhood."

"Get a Phil Donahue T-shirt instead."

He went into the master bedroom and opened the linen closet door. Her breath stalled as she watched him reach far inside and feel for something. His back straightened with surprise as he drew his hand out.

He held a box of shotgun shells and her diaphanous black robe.

Understanding and disgust slowly crept into his expression as he lifted the enticing garment for perusal. He turned slowly toward her, the robe looking fragile in his big hand.

"White used to be your color," he said succinctly.

"Don't draw analogies between my lingerie and my morals."

"Another gift from the banana king?"

Dinah lifted her chin proudly. "Since you're going to think the worst no matter what, I see no point in discussing it."

"Get that damned fur coat," he ordered in a rough tone. Dinah knelt beside the bed and reached underneath. She pulled the sable out and stood up.

"What are you going to do? Shoot it?"

"Bring it and come with me."

She followed him through the house to the kitchen, then out a door to the back porch. Damp, cold wind curled through the screens and combined with anxiety to make her shiver. From their charcoal grill Rucker got a can of lighter fluid and a pack of matches. He went to the outer door and swept a hand toward the dark, rain-drenched backyard.

She walked outside and waited. He angled ahead of her and they stopped on the matted lawn a few dozen feet from the house. He threw the robe down and pointed at the coat.

"I wanted to buy you something like that once, but you gave me a speech about the cruelty of trappin' animals for their fur."

Dinah smiled sadly. "And you said I made you feel so guilty that you couldn't look Jethro in the eye for a week. You told him not to worry—that possum skins were only good for decorating highways." She paused, and her smile faded. Dinah dropped the luxurious coat atop the robe. "This was a gift I couldn't refuse."

"Well, it's about to be a fried gift."

He doused both garments with lighter fluid, then lit several matches and threw them onto the pile. Blue-gold flames leapt into the air, and Dinah's nose crinkled at the smell of burning fur.

Her chest swelled with pride. This angry ceremony of

Rucker's gave her a sense of victory. Valdivia had forced her to wear these things; now Rucker was telling Valdivia to go to hell.

"Stop cryin' over it," he commanded. "I'm sure you know how to get another one from good old Diego."

She glanced at him in shock and saw that he'd been watching her face in the firelight. Dinah smoothed away the tear on her cheek. "Rucker, you don't know when to be quiet." She marched back inside.

Rucker proved that he did know when to be quiet. They left the house without speaking another word to each other, and the silence continued as they drove along a winding two-lane road. Rucker didn't bother to warn her when he suddenly swung the Land Rover off the blacktop. Dinah bounced hard and grasped the dashboard for support. They seemed to be heading into the middle of the woods. A second later the headlights illuminated a narrow dirt road overhung with skeletal oak trees.

"Where are we going?" she asked drolly. "And why didn't I bring my bear repellent?"

"Just relax and let me do the talkin'."

"I *never* talk to bears."

"Better to talk to bears than to Russian agents."

She clamped her mouth shut and vowed to speak only when necessary. There'd be less conflict that way.

A few minutes later the trees thinned and they entered a clearing. Dinah studied the ill-kept house and the car carcasses that dotted its front yard. A half-dozen baying hounds surrounded the Land Rover.

"Oh, no. No," she whispered with dread.

Two of them reared up and planted huge paws on her window. She made a guttural sound of panic and lurched frantically toward Rucker's side of the truck. Dinah collided with his right leg. Without thinking she reached for him with both hands. Her fingers dug into his denim-covered thigh.

He yelped in pain. "What the hell?" Rucker pried her hands away and held them hard. "You're shakin'. They're just old huntin' dogs. What's wrong with you?"

She gulped for air, and reason began to return. Dinah forced herself to move back to her side of the truck. "They startled me. They're so . . . loud."

"You always liked dogs. Even big dogs. You wanted a Labrador retriever."

Nerves turned into anger. "I've changed, all right? Just forget it."

He grasped her chin and forced her to look at him. Even in the dim light from the dashboard she could see his eyes probing her expression. "Does Valdivia keep dogs?" he asked gruffly.

She nodded. "Rottweilers."

His fingers tightened against her skin, but there was suddenly something gentle in his touch. "There's so much I don't understand. There's so much fear in you."

"The world isn't nearly the safe, wonderful place we thought it was."

"Why are you afraid of dogs now?"

His voice held a soothing quality that was new. Dinah quivered and reached up to stroke his hand. "Oh, Rucker," she whispered. "I wish . . ."

A rifle blast shattered the night. Rucker pushed her head into his lap, then bent over her protectively. He shoved his door open and yelled, "Dammit, Halfacre, calm down!"

They heard a high-pitched laugh. "Ain't used to gettin' visited in the middle of the night! McClure, you ugly jackrabbit, I wouldn't shoot nobody and you know it."

Rucker muttered darkly, "There's nobody who could star in a movie of Halfacre's life, because Walter Brennan passed away and Francis the Talking Mule ran off with a she-mule."

Dinah chuckled, then realized that her cheek was pressed against a denim-covered bulge that had begun to stiffen. Rucker realized the same. He sat up and she quickly followed. They avoided looking at each other.

"What you doin' here, jackrabbit?"

Rucker turned toward the squeaky voice. "Came to borrow one of your trucks for a few days."

Dinah peered past Rucker at the white-haired gnome who stood beside the truck wearing overalls and carrying a gun. The gnome smiled.

"I see you quit mopin' and got yourself a gal."

"Yep."

"How do, ma'am."

Dinah nodded to him. "How do."

"Boaz Halfacre, esquire. And what's your name, ma'am?"

"Lurleen," Rucker interjected solemnly. "Lurleen Studebaker."

"Same as the car?"

"Yes," she agreed. "My grandfather designed it."

"You rich?"

"See any Lurleens on the road lately?" Rucker inquired dryly.

Boaz laughed with explosive hee-hee-hees. Rucker swung his long legs to the ground and helped Dinah out through his doorway. The hounds milled around her legs, and she sidestepped them gingerly. Rucker moved close to her and put an arm around her waist. She forgot about the dogs and gloried in the affection he'd begun to show her.

"I want to put my Land Rover in your barn and use your old pickup for a few days, Bo. I'll pay. How does a hundred bucks sound?"

"Like honey from heaven. You got a deal."

"And if anybody comes by askin' questions, you never saw me." Rucker hesitated. "Or Lurleen."

"Never saw you."

Rucker drove the Land Rover into a ramshackle barn. They transferred their bags and the shotgun to a decrepit old pickup with peeling paint. Boaz put a rusty padlock on the barn door and tossed Rucker the key. The icy wind picked up and Boaz shuffled toward his house, Rucker's hush money clutched in his hand.

"Rucker McClure?" he called over his shoulder. "Never laid eyes on the boy."

Dinah studied Rucker lovingly as they went to their new vehicle. His stories had been peopled with real-life characters like Boaz, and he treated them with great respect. She wasn't surprised that he and the old codger were friends.

"How did you meet him?" she asked.

"I've taken to walkin' in the woods. I came up on his house one day. He nearly shot my head off. He's the last of the moonshiners."

They settled in the old truck. Dinah stared incredulously at its plush, sheepskin-covered seat and expensive stereo system, complete with tape deck. "What else does Boaz sell?"

"I never asked. It's none of my business."

"Can you trust him?"

Rucker looked at her sharply. "That's a fine question for *you* to ask."

Dinah settled on her side of the truck, tilted her head back on the seat, and shut her eyes. She tried not to feel wounded, but she couldn't help it. After the gentleness he'd shown her the new harshness was doubly painful, even though she deserved it.

Rucker started the truck and guided it back down Boaz's driveway. His silence grew oppressive. Dinah glanced at him anxiously and saw that his features had once again hardened with anger.

"Do you know what today is?" he asked.

She thought for a moment. "I think it's Tuesday. I've lost track."

"It's March twenty-sixth."

Dinah groaned softly. Today was their fourth anniversary.

Four

Dinah had her back turned toward the bedroom door, and she was busy fastening the lacy garter strap to her stocking. When she heard the door click shut softly, she smoothed her silk-sheathed leg and didn't bother to look around.

"Thanks, Millie. Just leave the milk on the dresser. I'll drink it in a minute."

"Bulls don't give milk," drawled a deep voice, smooth and sexy as warm bourbon.

Dinah whirled around. "*Sir,*" she said drolly, putting her hands on her hips, "You're supposed to be at the church."

"I got lonely. And I don't like to do what I'm supposed to do. You know that." Rucker stood there, a devilish but distracted smile on his face as his eyes roamed over her.

"How did you sneak past Millie?"

"I didn't. I'll have you know my tough little secretary's a romantic at heart." He paused. "And I promised her two extra days of vacation."

He wore a black tux with a white cummerbund. The white shirt had an old-fashioned wing-tip collar. He looked so handsome and gallant and utterly provocative that her knees went weak. He started toward her, his stride slow and purposeful, his body poised for action.

Laughing under her breath, she began to back away, tottering a little as the heels of her white pumps caught on the carpet. "It's bad luck for you to see me before the wedding."

"It's bad luck for me to see you in your weddin' dress," he corrected. His gaze moved down the low-cut bodice of her minislip to her garter straps and bare thighs. "Lord, Dee, that's not weddin' underwear. That's not proper at all."

Her face flushing with pleasure, she touched the slip's lacy hem. "I wanted to surprise you."

She kept backing, angling around the corner of the bed. He followed nonchalantly, knowing she couldn't run too far and that she didn't really want to escape. "Oh, I'm not surprised," he said in a low, gruff tone. "I've always known that there was a wild woman behind that southern-belle smile. Com'ere, Scarlett."

"Why, Rhett . . ." Dinah bumped into the wall beside the bed. Smiling, her chin up, she pointed to her intricately braided and upswept hair. "This took two hours. You *don't* want to be responsible for the damages."

He closed in on her, slid an arm around her waist, and pressed himself to her, gently pinning her to the wall. His mouth almost brushing hers, he murmured, "Our kids'll see the weddin' pictures some day and say, 'Momma, how come you look like a hen that's just been electrified?' And you can tell 'em that Daddy ruffled your feathers."

"As usual." Sighing with exaggerated defeat, she wound both hands into his hair and pulled him to her for a long, intimate kiss.

He drew his fingers up the center of her back. They slid across the nape of her neck, caressing languidly. Something cool trickled down the center of her chest and stopped just above her breasts. "Surprise," he whispered.

Dinah tucked her chin and gazed at the diamond and sapphire pendant that hung from a slender golden chain. "Oh, no."

"What?" he asked anxiously, and cupped her face between his hands.

"I'm going to ruin my makeup." She looked up at him with teary eyes. "But I don't care." Dinah kissed him tenderly, then put her arms around his neck and hugged him. "It's beautiful." She whispered into his ear, "Put your fingers between my breasts."

He drew back and gazed at her with feigned shock. "If I'd known jewelry would get me this much fun, I'd have given you some the night we met."

Dinah chuckled. He trailed one hand down to her breasts and gently slipped his forefinger into their warm valley. His eyes widened with intrigue. "You carryin' a bus ticket in case you get bored with the honeymoon? I don't think you can get a bus home from Acapulco."

"Be careful. It's pinned to my bra."

Thoroughly fascinated, he cocked his head and examined her bosom. Using both hands, he unfastened the small white envelope nestled between her breasts. "Hmmm, can't resist," he noted, then placed a kiss on the top of each one. He straightened, looking curiously at the envelope in his hand. Dinah stroked his shoulders and watched him with devotion. "You were supposed to find it later, but I can't wait. Open it."

He reached inside and retrieved the contents. An incredulous smile appeared beneath his thick mustache. "How did you get a pair of tickets to the Masters Tournament! *Nobody* can get these tickets! People wait for *years* to get tickets to the Masters!"

"The daughter of the tournament coordinator was a sorority sister of mine. I told her that my husband-to-be, the infamous Rucker McClure, loved golf more than anything in the world except me and grits. And that tickets to the Masters would be the best wedding present I could give him."

The look in his eyes was so loving that she gazed back in rapt silence, her mind blank and an awed little smile on her lips. He put his arms around her and studied her upturned face.

His low, gruff voice nearly melted her. "I take you to be my wife, to love and cherish, no matter what, for as long as I live. And afterward, too, if there's any way to arrange it."

She smiled wider at his somewhat practical rendition of the vows. "I take you to be my husband, to love and cherish, no matter what, for as long as I live. And afterward, too, because I'm sure you'll need someone to keep you out of trouble in heaven."

He sighed happily and brushed a kiss across her mouth. "You've got me, ladybug. You've got me for good."

"I'll never let you go," she promised.

Never.

"Never," Dinah whispered out loud. The sound of her own voice woke her from the uncomfortable half-sleep. The panic of disorientation, of waking too many times in too many strange and unpleasant places, jerked her eyes open in cold fear.

She sat in the floor on the truck's passenger side, her legs bunched against the door, her blue wool poncho wrapped around her. Overhead the windows let in the dim light of early dawn, and she glimpsed the tops of an oak grove. Rucker lay on his back on the seat beside her, his knees drawn up awkwardly.

He had his face turned toward her. The sight of him sleeping only inches away was another shock, but of a different sort. She was still desperate and vulnerable, but she wasn't alone anymore. *I love you so much,* she thought.

Thinking of nothing but that, she made a soft, keening sound of happiness and scrambled to her knees. Trembling, Dinah slowly joined her mouth to his.

For just a second his mouth remained relaxed in sleep, then its subtle tightening warned that he was groggily aware of her presence. Dinah was too reckless to stop; he would push her away at any moment, but she'd take as much of his affection as she could until then.

She nuzzled his mustache, then ran her tongue over his lips and pressed her mouth tighter to his. To her amazement his mouth became mobile, accepting, giving. A shiver of desire ran through her like wildfire.

His blue, quilted outdoorsman's coat was unsnapped. Dinah placed a hand, palm down, on his broad chest. The heat and hardness of it radiated through the soft plaid shirt. She stroked lightly, then lifted her hand to his throat, where she drew a fingertip along the ruddy skin.

She dipped down to the collar of his white T-shirt, where curly hair peeked out. Still kissing him, Dinah brushed her finger across that hair, remembering how many wonderful times she'd nestled beside him with her cheek against the tickling fur.

He inhaled roughly and stirred. Deep in his throat he made a small, primitive sound that was a pure masculine response to her touch. Dinah kissed his chin, his jaw, his forehead. She stroked his hair and studied his face with an almost reverent gaze.

Her other hand trailed lightly down his stomach to the waistband of his jeans. Oh, how he had loved her uninhibited caresses. So many times she had wakened him this way, her hands bawdy and her kisses delicate until he reached for her, eager to return the attention.

Dinah slipped her palm over the front of his jeans and found him eager now, though he still breathed with the languid rhythm of sleep. The slow heat of desire rose inside her, and her swollen breasts ached with sensations that only his hands could soothe.

Dinah rested her forehead against his. "Oh, honey," she mouthed silently. "I want you so much."

She knew that as soon as he woke up, which would be any moment now, he'd be angry with her. Trying to preserve the tenderness between them, she forced her hand away from his hardness. As her fingers skimmed over him she felt the angular imprint of the truck keys in his front pocket.

Dinah froze, her fingers resting on the forbidden item. She explored a little, and her breath stalled in her throat when she realized that the edge of the key ring protruded from his pocket. It would be so easy to steal the keys.

He wouldn't notice. When he woke up there'd be a good chance that he'd step outside of the truck for a minute. At which time, if she really loved him, she'd grit her teeth, crank the engine, and drive away without looking back. They were in the middle of nowhere, but they'd passed a small town a mile or two before stopping to sleep. He could walk there easily.

He'd never forgive her, but at least he'd be out of this dangerous predicament.

Sadness hollowed her inside as she caught the tip of her fingernail in the key ring and eased it out of his pocket. Dinah watched his face carefully for signs that he was waking. She slowly put the keys on the floorboard under the seat.

Now she looked at Rucker with the painful knowledge that she was going to leave him again, and soon. She'd do whatever it took to come back and bring their daughter with her, but he wouldn't know that.

Once more she touched him, and this time she unfastened his jeans, her fingers moving with great care. If she could give him this unselfish pleasure, perhaps he wouldn't be able to hate her.

His breathing quickened as she uncovered him, tugging his shirt tail up to reveal the tight, muscular abdomen she remembered so well. Dinah nestled her face in the crook of his neck and inhaled his masculine scent, trying to commit everything about him to memory. She eased her hand inside his jeans and stroked gently.

The feel of his smooth, rigid length against her fingers was so erotic that she moaned from bittersweet desire. They were right for each other in so many ways, not just this one, but it was all she could share with him on this cold March morning, their anniversary.

Suddenly his back arched. He strained against her wantonly caressing hand, hot and pulsing. Dinah anxiously drew her head up and looked at his face, dreading the moment when he would open his eyes and see her through a haze of anger.

His dark auburn lashes flickered. Dinah moaned softly and kissed him, dabbing her tongue to the center of his mouth seductively. A shudder ran through him and he twisted his mouth away from her.

Dinah wretchedly watched his eyes open. He looked up at her, blinking slowly, obviously stunned by what she was doing to him and his body's virile reaction. He stared at her tormented expression. A frown began to crease his forehead.

"No. No," she begged in a hoarse whisper. Dinah took his mouth before he could answer.

He gripped her shoulders as if to shove her away, but he groaned under the tantalizing assault of her mouth and hand. Dinah realized that his pleasure was so advanced that he couldn't ignore it.

She used the advantage, slipping her tongue into his mouth, making soft yearning sounds that drew a responding quiver through him. He shifted roughly in the small confines of the truck's cab, his body struggling under her touch. His hands rose to her long hair, twisting it, then grasping her head and holding it as he kissed her back.

The knowledge that she gave him so much pleasure made her bones dissolve. She was collapsing inside, falling apart in sweet sync with him. His head tilted back and his body pressed upward into her hand.

"Dee," he murmured hoarsely, as a wracking shudder signaled his release.

She cried then, hearing the old nickname for the first time. Dinah slid one arm under his neck and clung to him, her face burrowed in his shoulder while her hand feathered over his wet stomach.

His chest rose and fell harshly; his hands knotted in her hair then grasped her shoulders. He cursed in a soft, broken voice, then put his arms around her.

They were still and silent for a long time, caught up in the elemental sensations of holding each other again. Dinah feared that speaking would break the charm. She didn't even want to risk looking at him. With her head still resting against his shoulder, she reached out and fumbled with his clothes.

Her hand brushed over him intimately as she tucked his shirt and refastened the jeans. Rucker's embrace tightened.

"Why did you do it?" he demanded.

"Because you're still the only man in the world that I can't resist." Dinah raised her head and looked at him. "I don't have any ulterior motives. You've already agreed to help me, so why would I try to bribe you with sex?"

"Unless your conscience is botherin' you. I don't want you to touch me out of guilt."

"Oh, Rucker," she said with soft frustration. "It's not guilt." Dinah pulled one of his arms from around her. She guided his hand inside her poncho, then under her sweater and bra.

When his fingers touched one of her hard, wet nipples, a look of bewilderment came over his face. "Why is your milk comin' now?"

Dinah shut her eyes as exquisite sensations radiated from his touch. "It's a natural reaction to arousal. It happens to some women." She shifted forward, unable to resist the pleasure when his forefinger circled slowly.

"You're so warm and swollen. Does it hurt to be touched?" he asked in a barely audible voice.

Dinah gazed at him. His eyes were dark with emotion, but there was very little anger in them now. She smiled shakily. "It hurts good."

He slid his hand to the other breast and stroked it gently. "I guess you do want me," he murmured, studying her half-shut eyes and flushed face. His jaw stiffened. "How could you leave me last summer if you want me so much?"

Dinah frowned sadly and shook her head. "Don't. Don't ask questions like that."

He jerked his hand away from her and tugged her sweater back into place. "Time to hit the road again."

"Rucker—"

"I don't want to hear it."

He guided her away from him. Dinah sat on her heels and edged her fingertips under the truck seat. She found the keys and closed them in her hand.

Rucker straightened up and glanced at her, still sitting in the floorboard and gazing at him with an expression of regret. He abruptly put one hand under her arm and helped her rise to the seat.

"Thank you," Dinah said softly.

"Don't wake me up like that again, dammit."

"It wasn't premeditated." He put a hand on his front pocket. "Wait," Dinah interjected, her breath shallow. "I need a moment." She gestured out the window. "Don't you?"

"I can wait."

Dinah teased with hidden desperation. "When we went camping you thought it was a duty. A way to mark your territory and scare small animals."

Rucker eyed her ruefully and jammed his hand into his front pocket. He frowned as he searched it. "Damn."

"What's wrong?"

"The keys are gone."

"They must be here somewhere." That was true

enough. Dinah bit her lip and looked around vaguely, hating the deception. She clasped both hands in her lap.

Suddenly he grabbed her wrist. She jerked her gaze to his and saw suspicion in his eyes. They stared at each other for several seconds. The color rose in his face.

"You're losin' your expertise," he said in a strained tone. "When you're not with Valdivia you don't lie as well."

Dinah's shoulders slumped. She pulled her hand away, turned it palm up, and offered the keys along with quiet defiance. "I only wanted to do what was best for you."

Breathing harshly, he snatched the keys from her. "Everything you do is for somebody's good besides your own, isn't it? Just like a whore with a heart of gold."

She reeled inside. He'd always had a rough and colorful vocabulary, but in all their years together, he had never turned that vocabulary toward her with ugly intent.

Dinah gulped for breath and her stomach twisted sickly. She craved his trust and comfort; she'd dreamed of it to keep despair at bay. And now . . .

Her head snapped up. Her eyes glittered with anguished fury and her voice vibrated. "I didn't seduce you so that I could steal the truck keys when you were distracted. Don't you *ever* call me that name again. And stop acting as if you're the only one who has suffered."

Dinah shoved the truck door open and stumbled out. She sank to her hands and knees, fighting nausea.

Dimly she heard Rucker's booted feet hit the truck's running board as he climbed out after her. He knelt beside her and held her forehead in his wide, strong hand. The other hand clasped her waist, steadying her.

"I warned you to keep your distance," he reminded

her, but his voice was hoarse. "I also warned you that I could be cruel."

"I know. All right." She moved away from him and got wearily to her feet. He stood also, his hands clenched. Dinah waved him aside and climbed into the truck without help. He slammed the door.

By the time Rucker settled in the driver's seat, she sat facing forward with her shoulders squared. "I won't try to sneak away from you again. And I won't touch you again," she said with great dignity. "I swear it."

The roar of the truck's engine was the only answer she received.

Potsbog, Tennessee was so small that it made Mount Pleasant look like a metropolis, Dinah thought. They stopped at the town's one gas station and convenience store. Dinah went to the restroom, where she assessed her face in a mirror and estimated her age at about ninety-five.

When she went inside the store Rucker stood at the cashier's counter, a gasoline credit card in his hand. Dinah swept a gaze behind the counter and noted the computerized equipment with dismay.

She stepped close to Rucker, took the credit card from him, and smiled sweetly at the elderly man behind the cash register. "Excuse us, sir." He didn't smile back.

Rucker followed her outside, frowning. "What's wrong?"

Dinah returned the card and looked up at him grimly. "Jeopard undoubtedly has access to a computer network that will let him know the minute you use that. As soon as the clerk runs it through a credit check Jeopard can find out where we are."

After a stunned moment, Ricker's eyes narrowed. "I guess Valdivia trained you well."

Dinah nodded. "Just use cash. No problem."

"A problem. I have exactly ten dollars and I just bought

twenty dollars worth of gas. I didn't have time last night to get any extra cash, and I gave most of what I had to Boaz. I figured on using a bank card to get more."

"Checks?" she asked.

He shook his head. "Didn't bring my checkbook."

They shared a worried gaze. "The last thing we want is for the cashier to call the sheriff," Dinah noted.

"Let me handle this. I never met a country boy I couldn't reason with."

Drawing himself up, Rucker sauntered back inside. Dinah trailed after him.

"Friend, I've got a problem," he told the cashier jovially. "My wife forgot to pay the gas company this month and she says they'll pounce on my charge card like a duck on a june bug. And she spent most of my cash on a fancy breakfast this mornin'. I said, 'Edna, you don't need that extra side of ham.' But she's got an appetite like a fat nanny goat, so—"

"Boy, you ain't got enough to pay for your gas, and that ain't my problem," the cashier interjected. "That's the sheriff's problem."

"Please, sir," Dinah said quickly. "We need to get home to my sick mother, up in Kentucky. Have you got any work we could do to pay for the gas?"

"Nope."

"Has anyone in town got some work? We can do anything. My husband here, Bo, he's good with his hands."

"Either of y'all ever worked a diner? Cookin', waitin' tables?"

"Sure," they said in unison.

"Man down the street needs somebody this mornin'. His people didn't show up for work. Maybe he can help you. But that don't solve my problem."

Dinah lifted Rucker's arm and pointed to the heavy gold Rolex on his wrist. "We'll leave this as collateral.

And we'll let you hold the keys to our truck until we come back with some cash."

The clerk nodded. "I'll call the diner and see what I can do for you."

Minutes later, as they walked down Potsbog's main street toward a sign that said Eats Eats Eats, Rucker gazed at his watchless wrist. "I've got no use for fast-talkin' women," he grumbled mildly. "Especially smart ones."

Dinah eyed him with amusement. "When did you ever work in a diner?"

"Never. But my mother was the best truck-stop waitress in Texas. That ought to count for something. And I've eaten in more diners than a dog's got fleas." He eyed her back. "When did you?"

"I waited tables for a charity dinner at the country club once. When I was sixteen."

The desperate absurdity of the situation brought them together as nothing else could. As he opened a door posted Eats Eats Eats Welcomes You! No Pets! No Guns! Shoes and Shirts Must Be Worn! Rucker patted her on the rump and whispered, "Edna, good luck."

Dinah glanced over her shoulder and smiled. "Good luck, Bo."

The owner was a nervous man, Rucker could tell. He had a diner full of hungry people, most of them burly types who didn't waste patience on waiting for breakfast. And now he had a dedicated but bumbling waitress.

At least she was gorgeous. What man could care about food when she flashed that Miss America smile?

"Here. I'm confused. Just a second." She moaned under her breath and spread out a half-dozen order tickets on the long cutting board that fronted the grill. "This man wants his eggs over easy and still runny. No, that's over easy and well done. And this, this is an order for grits with cheese. Swiss cheese. No, American cheese. And this man wants cow toast. I understand world economics. Why can't I understand this?"

When she looked up from her frantic perusal of the tickets, Rucker saw wistful chagrin in her eyes. "What's cow toast?" she asked plaintively.

"You butter it, then broil it in the oven, instead of cookin' it in a toaster."

"Bless your heart." She lifted the hem of the coarse white apron she wore and dabbed at her perspiring face. She studied the deft way he shifted eggs, hash browns, ham, bacon, and steaks on the huge grill. "You look like you were born in a diner."

Rucker wiped a hand on his T-shirt, adjusted the white bandanna he'd wrapped around his forehead, and nodded proudly. "Almost was. Ma got off work and went straight to the hospital."

"Pretty Long Legs, can I have some more coffee, please?"

Rucker turned around and scowled at the big construction worker seated at the counter. "Her name's Din—Edna."

"Dinedna, can I have some more coffee, please?"

Rucker and she shared a droll look, and he wished suddenly that he could carry her out of this place to a private spot where they could make sense out of what was happening to them. "Hop to, Dinedna," he muttered.

She hurried to get a coffeepot, and he watched the determined, energetic way she moved. Whatever her secrets were, whatever truly motivated her, it worked well. She'd had very little sleep, she'd eaten only a package of cheese crackers for breakfast, and the morning had been decidedly traumatic. She was running on adrenaline and courage.

Katie. That's what drove her. Rucker drew a soft breath and went back to his work without concentrating on it. His wife had a baby, there was no doubt about that. But he had no way of knowing whether the baby was his or whether it was in danger.

He wanted to believe that the baby was his daughter, and that Dinah could explain why she'd left him last summer, and that she'd touched him out of love this morning. All he knew at the moment was that events during their separation had changed her, somehow hurt her, and had finally merged her strength with a compelling sense of purpose that he couldn't help but respect.

"Bo, save me!" Dinah Sheridan McClure, a highly intelligent and highly competent woman who knew all the Chopin piano etudes by heart and who read philosophy for fun, was beside him again, looking anxious. "What's a naked steak?"

He loved her. God, how he still loved her.

Five

"I never thought I'd be so happy over thirty dollars," Dinah admitted. "Minus ten for gas." She folded the remaining bills and tucked them into Rucker's shirt pocket, then leaned back on the truck seat and watched the Tennessee hills pass by.

"I was nineteen years old the last time I earned so little for so much work," he grumbled.

"Hmmm. Was that the summer you worked at the dog-food factory?"

"Yeah. I didn't have enough money to go back to college, but I had a lifetime supply of dog treats."

"You joined the Army that fall, didn't you?"

"Yeah."

"I was ten years old. I think that was the summer Mom and Dad took me to Europe."

"Lord, Dee, you and I are a strange pair."

His second use of her nickname subdued them both. Rucker's thick brows drew together in a pensive expression.

"Thank you," she said quickly. "I've missed it. You can even call me *Deedee*."

"Nah. You never liked *that*."

"I pretended not to like it."

"How many other things did you pretend about?"

Dinah inhaled sharply. Despite the companionable mood created by their morning's work, his anger and pain still lay just beneath the surface. She stared resolutely out the window.

"When are you gonna tell me where we're headed?" he asked in a grim tone.

"When we get there."

"Very funny."

"Did it ever occur to you that Jeopard may be listening to everything we say? It's unlikely, but possible. You wouldn't believe the sophistication of electronic listening devices—some are the size of postage stamps—and he could have put them in the seams of your clothes, your boot heels, your wallet. He'd plant bugs on you just in case I contacted you, and you'd never suspect it."

"You really think Jeopard's got me bugged?"

"Probably not. Otherwise, we'd be in custody by now. But I can't be certain. I won't risk it."

Rucker popped the truck into a lower gear as they hit a steep grade. The engine made a straining sound. 'Hope it's not all like this. We won't make it."

Dinah's reply was troubled. "We *have* to make it."

A half hour later, Boaz Halfacre's old truck climbed to a mountain plateau, decided enough was enough, and choked to a halt.

After inspecting under the hood, Rucker came back to the cab and muttered, "Jeopard, if you're listenin', you sneaky bastard, would you call Triple A?"

"What's wrong with the engine?"

"Probably the carburetor. I can't be sure, but if I had a decent toolbox I might be able to fix it."

Dinah stepped out, braced a hand on the door frame, and began to push. "Then we'll find someone who can loan us one."

"You've got the spunk of a blind ant tryin' to move an elephant. Take it easy."

She looked across the cab at him and said softly
"After you hold Katie in your arms, you'll understand."

His green eyes burned into her blue ones for a mo
ment. "Katherine Ann," he murmured pensively. "Al
right. I'm gonna believe in her."

Rucker put his shoulder against the door frame and
shoved the truck into motion.

The farmhouse was small, weathered, and inviting
It sat back from the road with towering mountains for
a background and a maple grove for close company. A
barn and other outbuildings surrounded it. A dozer
red-and-white Hereford cattle grazed in a pasture nearby.

By the time they pushed the truck up the rutted
gravel driveway, Dinah was panting and sweat ran down
Rucker's face despite the day's cool temperature.

A small, golden-haired woman walked out on the
front porch of the house, smiling shyly. She wore a
heavy beige sweater under a blue jumper. The jumper
ballooned over what must surely be an advanced preg
nancy. An anxious, aching emptiness stirred under
Dinah's rib cage. When she looked at the pregnant
woman's face, she knew that she wasn't much more
than a child herself.

"Hi, folks," the blonde said in a sweet voice laced
with an accent that made Rucker's sound cosmopoli-
tan. "Can I help y'all?"

Rucker cleared his throat and spoke politely. "Ma'am.
I'm Abe MacLane and this is my wife . . . Bethesda.
We're headed home from visitin' a sick relative in Nashville, and we've got engine trouble. Would you have a
toolbox I could borrow?"

"Sure!"

Dinah cocked a brow at him. Lurleen. Edna. Bethesda.
He was enjoying himself.

With a friendliness honed by rural self-reliance, the
young woman stepped gracefully down the porch steps

and headed toward a work shed. "Come on. I'll show you where my husband keeps things. Sam had to go to Nashville to buy some cattle and he won't be back until tomorrow. Sam Chase. And I'm Laurie. Nice to meet you. 'Scuse me if I waddle. I'm due in about two weeks."

Dinah and Rucker shared a strained look as they followed her. "Aren't you nervous way out here alone, with your baby about to be born?" Dinah asked.

Laurie used the toe of her tennis shoe to nudge a fat red hen out of their way. "Nah. Doctor says I shouldn't have any trouble."

"Aren't you goin' to a hospital?" Rucker asked.

"We're a little short of money for that. Besides, the hospital's two hours from here. My husband was born in this house. It's got sentiment to it."

They went into a small, neatly kept shed. She pointed to a tool chest. "There you go," she told Rucker.

"Thank you, ma'am."

He hoisted the chest and carried it outside. Guileless and curious, Laurie Chase smiled at Dinah. "If y'all want to stay awhile, I'll fix you a meal."

"We can pay," Dinah said quickly. "We don't want to impose."

"Hush. I'm happy to have company. Let's go in the house while your man works on the truck. You can help me cook."

She held out a hand, her eyes honest and sweet. Such innocence, Dinah thought sadly. She took the girl's hand and squeezed it. "That sounds good."

"I warn you, all I talk about is my baby."

Dinah smiled at her. "Me, too."

They sat by a window in the Chase's big, homey kitchen and peeled potatoes. Dinah watched Rucker work on the truck's engine. He occasionally took a swig from the cup of coffee she'd taken out to him.

"That's a good-lookin' stud hoss you got there," Laurie observed. "Bet he gave you a good baby."

Dinah bit her lip to keep from smiling at the girl's earthy description of Rucker. "He certainly did."

"Bet you hated to leave her with a sitter. I bet you miss her. Even for a few days. I bet you can't hardly stand it."

"Yes."

"I'm sorry. I can see from your face that I upset you. Ouch!"

Dinah looked up quickly. "Are you all right?"

The girl put a hand on her lower back. Her eyes widened. "That's the fourth time that's happened today. Like a weird kind of cramp. I shouldn't have carried so much firewood this morning."

Dinah excused herself and went outside. Rucker bent under the truck's hood, an array of hand tools spread around him. He was immediately aware of her; she could tell from the subtle tightening of his body. His wariness was both physical and emotional.

Gusting wind from a cloud-covered sky ruffled his hair, and his hands were greasy. His face was drawn with fatigue, and beard stubble covered his jaw, but somehow those things only made him more appealing. She knew that the rugged exterior hid depths of tenderness and passion. This was a man who would never let her see him cry over his own pain but who had once cried bitterly over hers.

Dinah stood beside him a second, watching him hungrily, inhaling the not unpleasant scents of oil, mountain air, and masculine sweat.

He finally glanced at her. "I'm hurryin', but it'll be a while."

"We can't leave right away. The girl's going into labor."

Rucker whacked his head on the truck's hood as he straightened up. "*What*?"

"I think she's going into labor. So don't hurry to fix the truck."

He gazed at her with a mixture of bewilderment and something else, something that made her chest swell with hope. "Rucker, I'm still the person who moves turtles out of the road so they won't get run over. I haven't become an ogre."

"You look exhausted. You gonna take on a stranger's problems, too?"

"Just this one's." Dinah gestured vaguely and glanced away, frowning. "If she's really going into labor . . . well, it's no fun to give birth alone."

"Were you alone?" he asked grimly, and his expression told her that the thought upset him.

"Basically, yes."

"Where . . . no. You can't tell me. I won't even bother to ask."

She nodded and faced him stoically, her heart twisting as she remembered how much she had needed him. "It's no fun," Dinah repeated.

"What's your schedule? Have we got time to stay and help?" he asked. His tone was softer, and there was grudging admiration in his eyes.

"Yes."

"Okay, then. It's gonna take me all afternoon to fix the truck, anyway." He paused, studying her. "Didn't anybody tell you that lady spies are supposed to be wicked and heartless? Don't you watch the movies?"

Dinah smiled wryly and nodded. She hugged herself against the cool wind and the shivering urge to lean forward and kiss him. "They're not supposed to love their husbands, either."

He flinched and started to lift his hands toward her. Dinah urged him with her gaze. His restraint was almost palpable, a force that conflicted with every beautiful memory she saw replayed in his eyes. After a tense second, the warmth faded from them. He lowered his hands wearily. "Spies can still love their husbands?"

"Yes."

"But then leave them without lookin' back? That takes pure meanness."

She felt his rejection as if he'd shoved her physically. "I looked back," she whispered. "Every step of the way." Dinah turned from the searing disbelief in his eyes and numbly went to the house.

A grandfather clock ticked in one corner of the Chase living room and fading afternoon light made the room shadowy. Good smells drifted from the stove in the kitchen. Laurie's monopoly on the conversation suited Dinah.

The girl rocked next to her, stroking a big orange cat that purred in her lap. Dinah let her own rocking chair remain still.

"Do you know who your husband reminds me of?" Laurie asked abruptly. "That writer. Rucker McClure."

Dinah jumped. She gathered her wits quickly and replied, "We've heard that before. He does look a little like him."

"I've got all his books. Wait, I'll show you."

Dinah straightened fearfully, searching her memory as the girl hoisted herself from the rocker and went to a nearby bookcase. How much did Rucker's publicity photograph resemble him? Laurie withdrew a slender hardback.

"This is the last one he wrote. It's my favorite. *Hot Grits and Honeysuckle*. About bein' married. It's got a lot of funny stuff about marriage in it, but you can tell that he really loves his wife."

The girl handed the open book to her and pointed at a photograph on the inside cover flap. "He's older lookin' than your husband and a little heavier. Plus he wears glasses. Look at that tailored jacket. Bet that tie's made of silk. He's a slick-lookin' devil. Not like your husband. I mean, that's a compliment."

Dinah sighed with relief and tried to smile. "I understand." Thankfully, she'd encouraged Rucker to dress up for the photograph. The glasses, which he used only for reading, were a last-minute addition. "Now I look like a man who likes poetry instead of *Sports Illustrated*," he'd grumbled.

"Go ahead and read some. I'll check on supper," Laurie told her.

As she left the room, Dinah lovingly smoothed a hand over Rucker's book. When she'd first met him, he wanted to write about her, but she was distrustful and frightened. Her past contained secrets that he might expose. It had taken a long time for her to understand that Rucker wanted to erase the past and give her a future.

Now she had to do the same, for him.

"Bethesda?"

She glanced around. "Hmmm?" Laurie Chase stood in the kitchen door, clutching the frame.

"My water broke."

Rucker rarely looked clumsy or ill at ease, regardless of the situation. "I feel about as graceful as a rhinoceros on a bicycle," he muttered tensely, as he bumped furniture and caught his boot toe on a braided rug.

"Relax, *Abe*. Everything's under control. Just put that floor lamp close to the bed." Dinah looked down at Laurie and patted her hand. "So the doctor says you have a wide pelvis. Good. Me, too. And I didn't have any trouble."

The girl's eyes fluttered shut. "I wish Sam was here to hold my hand."

Rucker set the lamp down and plugged it in. "I'm good at hand holdin'."

"I'd like that, Abe."

He gingerly sat down by her pillow and grasped the small, calloused hand she raised. "You just hang on to my big ol' paw and everything'll be all right, missy."

Dinah's chest tightened at the gentleness in his voice and face. She cleared her throat and smiled at Laurie. "I used to . . . I call him the human tranquilizer. If you close your eyes and listen to his voice, all your worries will float away."

"He has a moose voice," Laurie observed solemnly. "If a moose could talk, he'd sound like Abe."

"Stop. I'm shy," Rucker protested.

The girl winced as a new contraction hit her. "Talk to me, Abe. I know, tell me how you and Bethesda met. I love stories about stuff like that."

Rucker's gaze rose to Dinah's. They shared a strangling look of sorrow. "I'll go put supper away," Dinah said quickly. "And clean up the kitchen. And I'll, hmmm, feed the cat and the chickens. Abe can tell you all about us."

She hurried out of the room.

They leaned against the back of the garden bench, kissing each other slowly and thoroughly.

He held her and she nestled her head into the crook of his neck. Rucker rested his cheek against hers, his mustache brushing her skin. Under her cool, intellectual exterior was a woman who secretly wanted to have someone rough up her smooth edges, he realized. And he was the perfect man to do the roughing.

"This is a helluva fantastic first date," he told her in a low, teasing voice.

"This isn't a date," she argued. "It's . . . I don't know what it is."

"But you know what it's gonna lead to if I hang around your town a few more days."

"I have a vague idea. I make no guarantees."

But he heard a yearning tone in her protest. Rucker mustered all his restraint to keep from tilting her head back and kissing her longer, deeper, and slower than before.

"Want me to leave?" he asked.

"Would you leave if I asked you to?"

"Of course not."

She laughed, sounding resigned but not very upset. "Then I might as well not ask."

"I sure am glad you're so smart."

"There's nothing smart about this. Two people who barely know each other, who are so different—"

"Who need each other," he countered. "Who fit together like two spoons in a tray. Who knew that the first night they laid eyes on each other."

"I laid eyes on a man with a possum on his head."

Rucker sighed confidently. "I'm just perfect. I admit it." He chuckled, loving the exasperated sigh his comment provoked from her. After a second she began to laugh, too.

"I think 'unique' would be a better description, Mr. McClure." She paused, then slid one hand across his chest and patted the area over his heart. "Special," she amended softly.

Rucker shook off the memory of that night as Laurie's whimpering cries of pain became louder. He hadn't told her anything remotely true about his and Dinah's early courtship. He made up a story, and because he was a master storyteller, she listened and believed. Rucker smoothed a hand over the girl's damp forehead. Where was Dinah? She'd been outside for more than thirty minutes.

"Were you with Bethesda when she had y'all's baby?" Laurie asked in a weak tone.

Rucker inhaled raggedly and was glad that Laurie had her eyes shut. He was sure that his expression would puzzle and frighten her. "No, I wasn't."

"W—why? She loves you so much, and you're so s—sweet."

Rucker squeezed the girl's hand and thought bitterly, *I don't know if she loves me or not. She didn't want me to be with her.*

He heard a door open elsewhere in the house. "I'll be right back, missy," he promised.

"H—hurry."

Rucker walked quickly down a hall to the kitchen. Dinah closed the door to the back porch and looked up as he stepped into the room. She frowned comically and pointed to a speck of blood on her wrist.

"I've just had my first encounter with hungry chickens. No one told me that chickens are carnivorous."

"Something's happenin' with Laurie," he told her. "Come on. I'm no good at this. I watched my dog have puppies once, and I nearly fainted."

Dinah threw her wool poncho on a chair, then ran to the kitchen sink and began scrubbing her hands. She smiled. "But you're a grown man now."

"Hell, I was thirty-two *then.*"

The look she gave him was both amused and reassuring. "Go help Laurie sit up. Let her brace her back against you. I'll be there in a second."

He turned to leave, then hesitated. "Dee?"

"Yes?"

The anger inside him wouldn't let the thought rest. "I wish to God I'd been with you when Katie was born."

The understanding and sorrow that flooded her eyes shook him to the core. "My darling, I wanted you there more than you can ever imagine."

A little stunned, he simply nodded.

Samuel Chase Jr., was born that evening just after ten o'clock. Both mother and son fared well, and by eleven young Sam was cleaned, fed, and wrapped in a blue baby blanket that had belonged to several generations of the family.

Dinah and Rucker left him asleep by his mother's

side. They walked wearily to the kitchen and slumped at the table. Dinah put her head on her folded hands.

Abruptly she felt Rucker's strong, supple fingers on the back of her neck. "Good work, gal," he murmured. "I was a great coach, but you were a star quarterback."

His touch produced incredible sensations in her tired muscles. "We make a terrific team," she agreed groggily, then chuckled. "Even if you did keep saying *shove* instead of *push*."

He laughed too. "*Push* didn't do the trick. Not tough enough."

"Wasn't it wonderful?"

Rucker laughed again. "Different from puppies." His laughter trailed off and his voice became serious. "Yeah. Even when you know all the biology about it, it still seems like a miracle—that little life growin' from the love two people share."

"When I held Katie the first time, right after she was born, I kept thinking, 'Rucker and I are together inside this tiny person. Nothing can ever change that. We created a new life that will always hold a part of us.' It *was* a miracle, because I felt so close to you even though you were thousands of miles away."

She shut her eyes in a grimace of remorse as his fingers quivered against her skin. She sensed all his anguish and unanswered questions. Both she and he were silent for a few seconds. His voice came to her, low and troubled. "Did you hurt as bad as Laurie did?"

"I've forgotten how much. Mother Nature has a way of erasing the memory. But yes, it hurt."

"You didn't have any painkillers?"

"No."

"A doctor?"

"In the Suradoran jungle? No. A midwife. An Indian woman who'd been trained in nursing."

Rucker's voice became tense. "Wasn't that a risky way to have our baby?"

"I didn't have any choice."

She heard his harsh intake of breath. "Because of Valdivia?"

"Yes."

Rucker withdrew his hand. "So you always let him tell you what's best?" he asked in disgust.

Dinah struggled for a moment. What else could she say? "Yes."

"That's a helluva cowardly way to live. I'm not sure which I hate worse—you bein' a traitor to your country or bein' a slave to a man like Valdivia."

Dinah flinched. Their momentary truce had left her open and vulnerable to his attack. She was so tired. So tired of the fear, the loneliness, the worrying about Katie, the hurting for Rucker, the hurting for herself, so tired of the stomach-wrenching frustration from hiding the truth. She couldn't take anymore of Rucker's painful insinuations, deserved or not.

She raised her head, heedless of the big tears that slipped down her cheeks. His harsh gaze was on her. "I know you like being cruel to me," she said brokenly. "And I understand why. But please, for just a little while, stop trying to make me hurt worse than I already do. It's too much right now."

She stood, swayed a little, then went to the sink and splashed water on her face. Her whole body ached with fatigue. Dinah put her elbows on the sink's edges and leaned gratefully on the support, her head bowed.

To her horror, new tears insisted on finding their way to the surface. She bit her lower lip and dug both hands into her hair in a vain attempt to control the tremors that ran through her. She heard him rise and step close beside her.

"Dinah."

"N—no. Don't say anything else right now!"

"Dee."

"No!"

"Dammit, woman."

He grabbed her harshly by the shoulders, then turned

her toward him. Dinah saw the torment in his face and put her hands against his chest defensively. He cursed and jerked her to him.

Rucker slid one hand around her waist. The other cupped her head and pulled it to his shoulder. Amazed, Dinah stood stiffly within his embrace, her eyes wide. Then she groaned softly and sagged against him, unable to resist the warmth and strength she had craved for so many months.

"Words aren't very safe between you and me right now," he told her gruffly. "So let's just be quiet."

"That would be wonderful."

They needed each other on an elemental level that sought solace and understanding through touch. Dinah put both arms around his back and held him tightly, loving the heat and hardness of his big body. She felt muscles contract under his soft plaid shirt as her hands stroked him from shoulder to hip.

She wanted to tantalize his senses until he realized that they still shared the same life force; the same goals, the same dreams. She wanted to reeducate him, body and soul.

Dinah slid her hands down his thighs and pulled his pelvis snuggly against her, finding the hard ridge she had expected. She heard his breathing rasp against her ear. Her knees turned weak as pleasure flared from every inch of contact.

Suddenly he twisted her sideways, reached underneath her legs with one muscular arm, and lifted her off the floor. She looked into his eyes and saw the heavy-lidded hunger of a man who'd slept alone for many months. He hadn't soothed his needs with another woman; she didn't have to ask to know that such consolation would have been contrary to everything that was loving and loyal in his nature.

She returned his hunger with equal measure. Dinah tilted her head up and caught his mouth desperately, making him groan with surprise. She slid her tongue into his damp heat, tasting him wantonly and teasing without restraint.

He made a thick sound of torment and surrendered, his tongue gliding over hers and penetrating the responsive intimacy she offered. Dinah arched against him, her breasts so hot and full that the contact with his broad chest was nearly painful.

"Just let me," she murmured raggedly, nuzzling his mustache. "Just let me have a chance."

His chest rose and fell harshly. Rucker raked her with a dark look full of need and conflict. Silently he turned and carried her into the living room.

The fire burned low there, barely keeping the dark night at bay beyond the room's windows. Rucker sat down, still holding her, in an overstuffed chair near the crackling embers. Dinah studied the harsh shadows playing on his face and hoped that they were only the fire's illusion. She put her arms around his neck and began to pull his head toward hers.

"No." He bit the word off curtly. Rucker angled his legs so that her rump settled between them. Dinah's feet hung over the chair's fat armrest. He withdrew his arm from under her and tugged her arms from around his neck. Rucker covered her hands with a grip that was almost fierce.

"No more," he ordered.

Dinah looked up into his hooded eyes and realized sadly that the harshness had been real. "I won't hurt you," she whispered.

"The hell you won't." His breathing was rough, his body taut with resistance. "This is one barrier I won't let down. I'm doin' my best not to let you rip me apart again."

Her body went slack as desire faded. Dinah wearily pulled her hands away. "Then what are we doing in the same chair?"

"Playin' by *my* rules, for once. If you want to sleep,

then sleep. That's all. I'll listen in case Laurie needs us."

Dinah took several steadying breaths. Wasn't it enough for the moment to be this close to him? And even his reluctant intimacy was a good sign. Slowly she rested her head against his shoulder. To her amazement, exhaustion overwhelmed her as if she'd pushed a button.

Life would soon be good again. She was back with her husband, and his bitter words didn't hurt too much because he curled his arm around her shoulders. He even let one bristly cheek lay against her forehead.

"Love you," she murmured, just before her breathing slowed and her hands relaxed into her lap. Her last second of awareness centered on the movement of Rucker's lips as he formed a silent, secret response.

Six

Sam Chase Sr., a lanky, friendly faced redhead, arrived home at dawn and was thoroughly stunned to find his wife in bed with their new son at her breast. His work-scarred hands fumbled nervously as Rucker handed him the baby.

After Sam Senior nearly dropped Sam Junior, Rucker took the infant back and offered some man-to-man instructions on "baby wrangling."

"Put one hand under his head and one hand under his butt," Rucker explained solemnly. "And don't get the two ends confused. That's all there is to it."

Dinah cornered him in the kitchen a few minutes later. "I see that you've become an expert," she noted, smiling.

"Well, I rocked Sam Junior half the night. I earned my credentials."

Dinah studied Rucker's pensive expression and distracted gaze. "What are you thinking?" she asked softly.

He raised his hands in supplication and nodded vaguely toward the Chase's bedroom. "Holding the baby. Made me think of Katie. I felt paternal. Protective. Strong." He paused, frowning. "And impatient. Let's hit the road."

She nodded, her eyes shining. "You're a father now. Once you see Katie, you'll understand the feeling even more."

His gaze hardened. "When will that be? When will we go to South America?"

Dinah gave him a slow, incredulous stare. "Do you honestly expect to go back with me?"

"Honesty doesn't have much to do with our relationship right now."

"Rucker, no." She reached out, gripped his shirt front, and shook her head firmly. "*No*. You never cease to astonish me. I'm leaving you here in the States. You're not coming to Surador."

"How are you gonna stop me?"

Dinah emphasized each word. "Do you want to put your life in danger?"

"Tell Valdivia that I'm not meddlin' in his work. I'm only interested in bringin' my daughter home."

A little shaken, she asked miserably, "And your wife?"

"You have a choice. Katie doesn't." He pivoted away from her and stared out the kitchen window. The golden light of sunrise washed over him, illuminating his grim face. "You say that you always planned to come back to me. When? The only reason you showed up on my doorstep two days ago was because you needed money."

"I planned to come home after this mission."

"What's special about this one?"

"It's the end of a project. Valdivia won't need me anymore."

A muscle worked in his jaw. "So you were gonna waltz back home and pick up where we left off . . . until you decided to desert me again."

"I won't ever leave you again," she said hoarsely. "I swear it." She touched his back and found the muscles rigid with tension. "Rucker, you can trust me. You have to let me finish this job by myself." She smiled sadly. "It's a package deal, partner. You get me *and* Katie. But on my terms. That's the way it has to be."

His strained voice was barely audible. "Did it ever occur to you that I might not want you?"

Dinah stepped back, clutching a counter edge for support. "Don't say that! You don't mean it!"

"You're overlookin' a key problem. Your cover's been blown. You're a felon. You gonna come back to the States with our baby and spend the rest of your life hidin'?"

The blood drained out of her face and her lips parted in wordless pain. Finally she managed to say, "I'm innocent. And I plan to prove it." Dinah blinked rapidly, feeling stricken. "I never thought that you might not want me anymore."

He cursed softly and shut his eyes. His arms were braced rigidly on the kitchen sink. "You've built a life full of secrets. *How the hell can you prove that you're innocent?*"

"I can't tell you that—"

Rucker whirled toward her, his eyes fierce. "Exactly. Nothing you've done makes a damn bit of sense. I don't care how you explain it. Everything we shared is gone. It might as well have happened to two different people. I've changed. You've changed. Maybe we can't ever go back."

She gazed at him in growing despair as understanding stabbed through her. "All the suffering, all the uncertainty. All the bitterness you've felt toward me. My explanations may not matter. It'll be hard for you to forget."

"How could what you've done ever be forgotten? Hell, how can I know what to think when you won't tell me anything? All I know is that I *am* goin' to South America with you. I *am* goin' to get my daughter. There's no point in discussin' it."

Dinah gazed up into the icy determination that etched his features. Arguing would only jeopardize her mission and make him distrust her more. But she'd never let him follow her into Valdivia's clutches.

"There's a small part of you that hates me," she whispered. Dinah looked away so that she wouldn't see that observation confirmed in his eyes. She watched her fingers turn white from gripping the counter edge.

Rucker inhaled roughly. His problem was precisely the opposite. He couldn't hate her, he wanted her back desperately, and the knowledge that he was a fool for feeling that way was almost more than he could stand. Don't manipulate me for sympathy. Don't try to get inside me. What I feel about you is none of your business."

"That's no answer. You're deliberately being vague."

"It's the best answer you're gonna get. And don't talk to me about being *vague*."

The blankness that came over her was oddly welcome after months of anxiety and sadness. Dinah gazed up at him again while apathy washed away all expression from her face. Only a dull inner recess of her mind registered the fact that concern filled his eyes as he scrutinized her.

"You'll love Katie even if you can't love me anymore," she told him in a flat tone. "And whatever happens to me, she'll be free, and home, and safe. That's all that matters."

She turned and left the room with her shoulders squared, as if everything she'd dreamed about hadn't just begun to crumble around her.

Minutes after they crossed the Kentucky state line, light snow began to fall.

"Lovely spring weather," Rucker noted. He flipped the windshield wipers on and glanced at Dinah. A fast-food container lay unopened in her lap. Her hands cupped the food box loosely, so still that they might have been carved from stone.

"You need to eat," he commented.

"I'm not hungry. She placed the container next to

him. "Here. The way you wolfed your lunch down, I know you must be starving. Take mine, too."

"You haven't had anything but coffee all day."

"We don't have much farther to go. A couple of hours. Maybe I'll eat then."

"You're runnin' on empty and you're gonna be sick." Rucker let anger mask his growing alarm over her lifeless attitude. His voice rose. "How the hell are you gonna do what you need to do if you don't take care of yourself?"

"I have reserves of strength that I never imagined," she replied calmly. "The past months have taught me that."

He guided the truck to the grassy roadside and jerked it into park. Rucker removed the hamburger from its container and thrust it toward her. "We're not movin' another inch until you eat."

She surveyed him nonchalantly and shrugged. "You win."

He watched her dutifully bite into the sandwich. Rubbing his temples, he wearily leaned back in the seat. After a moment he turned the radio on. Dionne Warwick's voice purred the poignant, lost-love lyrics of "A House Is Not a Home."

Rucker suppressed a grimace and snapped the radio dial to another station. Dinah made a choking sound. He looked over to find her setting the half-eaten hamburger on her knee. The unspoken pain was between them. The song had hurt.

"That's all I can take," she said in a small voice.

"Finish it."

Her unfathomable expression never changed. Moving with slow grace, as if she were doing nothing out of the ordinary, she opened the truck door and tossed the hamburger out. She shut the door, clasped her hands in her lap, and faced forward primly.

"You're messin' with the wrong man," Rucker said in a soft, lethal tone.

"I don't want anymore to eat."

He put the truck keys in his pocket, got out, walked casually around to her side of the vehicle, and picked the hamburger up. Carefully he brushed little bits of twig and grass from it. Then he wrenched her door open and held the hamburger to her lips.

"*Eat it*," he ordered.

Color rose in her face. "Absolutely not." He sank one hand into her thick brunette hair and held her head still. Astonished, she grabbed at his wrists and tried to push his hands away. "Why do you care if I eat or not! No! Rucker . . ."

Her next words were muffled by the sandwich he deftly shoved between her teeth. She struggled, her body writhing with anger, and inadvertently took a large bite.

He pressed the heel of his hand under her chin and clamped her mouth shut, then smiled coldly at her throaty growl of dismay. "You've got no choice but to chew and swallow. This is how a vet gets medicine into an ornery cat."

She arched a brow at his tactic, her eyes flaring with humiliation, but she chewed. Eventually, she swallowed. He released her chin and dabbed the remaining bite of hamburger against her mouth. "Over the lips and past the gums, look out belly, here it comes," he chanted sardonically. His hand tightened in her hair, tilting her head back a little more.

Dinah sighed in resignation and opened her mouth. At exactly the right moment, when his blunt fingertips were brushing her lower lip, she lunged forward and caught them between her teeth.

"Dammit, Dee!" He jerked his hand away and looked at the trails her teeth had left in the pads of his fingers. His disgruntled gaze rose slowly to her satisfied one. She chewed and smiled.

Rucker couldn't help feeling proud of her. "At least you're not actin' like a wilted flower anymore. It's good to see the old fire."

"I'm not causing you any trouble. Don't complain."

"No trouble?" he repeated drolly. "Lady, you wrote the book on causing me trouble."

"I'll be out of your life soon, if that's what you want."

Because she'd provoked him, and because he was tormented by conflicting needs to comfort and punish her, he retorted, "That's the best promise I've heard all day."

He shut her door and strode back to his side of the truck. When he was seated behind the wheel, he found her gazing out the window again, locked in her silent, subdued world.

Rucker slammed on the brakes and instinctively threw his arm across Dinah's body to protect her from the sudden momentum. She latched both hands onto his forearm. They both stared wordlessly at the roadblock in the distance.

Two Kentucky state patrol cars were angled across the narrow two-lane road, leaving only enough space for a vehicle to pass between them. Two officers stood by the window of a station wagon, apparently checking the driver's credentials.

"Could just be routine," Rucker noted grimly.

"Looking for expired driver's licenses and proof of insurance," she agreed, her breath short. "Or they could be looking for us. Damn. We're only an hour away."

Rucker put the truck in reverse and guided it in a smooth about-face. "We'll try to find a detour."

He gunned the engine and sent the old truck hurtling back the way they'd come. Dinah twisted in the seat and watched behind them, her heart pounding. "We were so close," she said in a low, frustrated tone.

"Then you ought to tell me where we're headed."

She hesitated, then offered quietly, "Near Patula."

"There's nothin' near Patula but national forest land."

"And a few homes that were allowed to remain after the government bought the land."

His brow creased with thought. "Isn't that where Dr. Scarborough had a second home?"

Dinah silently cursed her decision to give him information. "Can't you drive any faster?"

A stunned expression came over his face. "Are we goin' to see Anna Scarborough?"

Dinah grimaced in self rebuke as she kept her vigil at the truck's back window. She had said too much, too soon. "Just drive."

"What have you and that eccentric old lady got to do with each other?"

"Who said we're going to see Anna Scarborough?" she demanded anxiously, her voice rising. Dinah thought she heard the faint wail of a siren. Her palms sweating, she grasped the back of the seat and strained her eyes watching a bend in the road behind them. "That 'eccentric old lady' is a reknowned biologist," she reminded Rucker.

"And that's who we're goin' to see? Why?"

"I never said . . ."

Her voice trailed off as they both heard the siren. It was closing on them quickly. Dinah turned toward Rucker and placed trembling hands on his shoulder. "We have to get off this road. Anywhere."

"Hold tight. There was a loggin' trail . . . there!"

He swung the truck to the right down a slope covered in an inch of slick snow. It slid into the snow-frosted ruts of the old road and bounced roughly.

"So much for the shock absorbers," Dinah joked grimly.

They careened into the depths of a hardwood forest, the truck's wheels spewing damp earth and humus. "We'll follow this as long as it goes," Rucker told her. His big hands fought the steering wheel as the truck slid sideways, slapping against low tree limbs.

Dinah swallowed hard and gazed at the wilderness all around them. "The patrol must have gotten a good look at the truck. If they weren't after it before, they'll be after it now."

"But they didn't see *us*."

Dinah laughed tonelessly and rubbed her forehead. "So we'll just call a taxi. Or wait for the bus. Or catch the subway."

"Or whine and give up."

"Never." She sat back and crossed her arms over her chest.

"I knew *that* would singe your hackles."

After about two miles the road came to an abrupt end in a small clearing. They let the truck idle and sat silent for a moment. Snow feathered down soundlessly.

"We walk," Rucker volunteered. "North. Until we intersect the main road beyond the road block. And then we hitch a ride."

"Before nightfall," she said adamantly.

"Woman, you're greedy." There was a slight teasing tone in his voice. She almost smiled.

They got out and gathered their canvas bags from under a tarp in the back of the truck. Rucker tucked the shotgun in the crook of one arm. "Keep your eyes peeled. And try not to scream if you see a wild pig. I've heard that they're all over the place up here."

Dinah busied herself trying to arrange her bag like a backpack. Distracted with worry over their situation, she blurted, "After Valdivia, nothing makes me scream."

She regretted the revealing words immediately. Rucker's expression turned dark with intensity. "How did Valdivia make you scream?" he asked in a low, horrified tone.

His concern brought unshed tears to her eyes. Dinah shook her head, struggling for control of her tight throat. Finally she managed to say, "I believe you *could* love me again, if you tried."

They reached the top of a hill and stopped for a second. Dinah brushed a tendril of snow-dampened hair back from her face and gazed wearily at the broad, wooded valley before them. "Rucker, I don't think we're going to intercept that road anytime soon."

"Dammit, just keep goin'.."

His voice was almost vicious. Startled, she looked at him anxiously. He stood a dozen feet away, his legs braced apart and his expression dark. He yelled at her with suddenly unleashed grief and frustration. "Why did you leave me?"

She started backing away, her eyes full of tears but her chin up. "Don't start that again, not now. We have too many other things to worry about . . ."

"I want an answer—I want the *truth*!" He leaned the shotgun against a tree and threw his canvas tote off his shoulder. Then he strode toward her. "An answer," he commanded harshly. "I won't play by your rules anymore! If you want my help, then you better talk!"

"You wouldn't believe the truth right now! And it would only complicate things! Put you in more danger!"

The ground made an ominous sound under his boots, as if a heavy piece of wood were cracking. "I'd rather be in danger than in hell—which is where I've been for the past ten months! Talk!"

She made a strangled sound of utter defeat. "All right, all right! I was—"

The ground gave way beneath him in a wrenching collapse that upended rotten boards and timbers like the broken bones of some strange animal. Dinah screamed as he disappeared into the maw of the violent earth.

Seven

Dinah ran to the side of the gaping hole, which was easily six-feet wide. She succumbed to a sense of terror unlike anything she'd ever felt for herself. She dropped to her knees and gripped the edge of a timber.

"Rucker!" Her voice was as jagged as the torn wood.

He was pinned about fifteen feet down in the corner of what appeared to be the entrance to an old gem mine. Several thick timbers were jumbled over his legs, but he sat upright with his back jammed against a wall shored with rotting planks. His head drooped forward.

"Please God, let him be all right," Dinah whispered. "Rucker!"

He raised his head slowly, gasping for breath, then nodded to show that he'd heard her. His face was drawn with discomfort.

"Hold on," she told him. "I'm coming down!"

Dinah threw one leg over the edge of the hole and pushed tentatively at a long timber that angled to the bottom. It seemed sturdy.

"Don't try it!" he called. "Everything else might collapse!"

She hesitated, struggling to control the reckless impulse that made her think only of going to him quickly. "Are you hurt?"

"Nothing a Band-Aid couldn't fix." He struggled fiercely for a moment, and his helpless torment wrung a cry of despair from her.

Heaving for breath, he halted the vain effort and looked up at her wearily. "My legs are trapped."

She looked down into the dark shaft and shivered for him. Dinah didn't have to ask to know that the ground underneath him was cold and probably damp. A furious sense of determination hummed in her veins. She had to get him out of that horrible gravelike hole.

"I'm going for help!"

His grime-covered face became terribly haggard looking. "Don't lie—this is the chance you've been waitin' for. You won't be back."

Her mouth gaped in horror. "You're wrong."

Rucker laughed humorlessly. "Go on. But have the decency to tell somebody where to find me before I catch pneumonia."

Bitter disappointment made her head droop in defeat. If he truly believed that she could leave him there to suffer, then little was left of the love he'd once felt for her.

"I'll go for help," she repeated dully. "I give you my word. If you don't want to believe in it, that's your problem." She frowned with concentration, thinking. "There's a rope behind the seat in the truck. I'm going to get it. Maybe I can drag these timbers off of you somehow."

"You can't budge these things. Just go. Get the hell out of here. I don't expect any loyalty from you."

She shook her head in exasperation. "I'd like to come down there and punch you."

They looked at each other in silence, his gaze furious and hers challenging. Dinah ignored the insult in his attitude and told him staunchly, "It'll take me nearly an hour to walk back to the truck—two hours, round trip."

His voice was wary. "I won't hold my breath."

"Good. Blue isn't your color." She vaulted to her feet. "I'll leave the shotgun with you. I'd probably just fall and shoot myself in the toes."

He scowled at her. "Take it. Remember the wild pigs I told you about?"

She chuckled ruefully. "The only wild pig I'm concerned about is you. I'm not leaving you trapped in this pit with no way to protect yourself."

"I'll be all right if you keep your word and come back."

Dinah groaned in disgust and warmed the air with several colorful oaths she'd learned from him over the years.

She retrieved the shotgun and removed the shells. Then she lay on her stomach by the collapsed mine and gingerly dropped the gun into his upraised hands. The shells followed. Dinah winced as she noticed that he was already shivering. She pulled the wool muffler from around her neck and tossed it to him.

"Cover your thick skull." She tried to joke. "And call down to the front desk. Tell the manager you'll be checking out of this crummy hotel soon."

"Not me. I ordered a chicken dinner from room service." He held the muffler in one big hand and looked up at her with troubled eyes. "Just tell me this. What were you goin' to say when I was comin' toward you a few minutes ago?"

She smiled pensively. "Sorry. You missed your chance. Believe me, I know what's best for you to know and not know."

His jaw worked as he sought to control his new frustration. He stared away from her and his tone became lethal. "Just turn around and start walkin'. Don't look back. You ought to be good at that."

She gazed at him miserably, nodded, and left.

• • •

He appeared beneath the oak tree as if the mountains had magically set him in her path—without sound, without warning. The black-haired giant might have been some ancient warrior unleashed by a wizard's spell. He had a long beard. From her perch on a low limb, Dinah stared down in amazement.

He swung his thick walking staff as if he were hitting a golf ball—only the end of the staff connected with the haunch of a grunting wild boar. The animal squealed in alarm and disappeared into a snowy thicket.

The giant tilted his head back and gazed up at her unemotionally. She held a noose of rope in one hand. "What were you going to do?" he inquired in a deep voice devoid of any discernible accent.

"Lasso him and tie him to a limb so that I could get down."

"And then?"

"Think of some way to get my rope back."

"Good plan, except for the last part."

Dinah studied him shrewdly. This huge man might be their ticket out of trouble or he might be trouble personified. She gritted her teeth.

"I need help. My husband fell into an old mine shaft. Up that way." She pointed.

"How far?"

"About thirty minutes from here."

He held up a massive hand. "Come down, please. I'll go with you."

His politeness offset his threatening appearance. Dinah knew that she couldn't escape from him, regardless of whether he was friend or enemy. Trusting instincts that had saved her more than once during the past ten months, Dinah tossed him the rope and scrambled down from the tree.

Rucker held his wristwatch overhead so that it caught

the dim afternoon light. She'd been gone nearly three hours.

He groaned from much more than physical discomfort. Could she really do it? Walk away and leave him again, this time in a dank prison with the cold numbing his trapped legs?

No. She couldn't do that to him. He had to believe in the woman he'd lived with, made love to, and cared for—the woman who'd cared for him in return. Shivering, he leaned his head back on the muddy plank wall and tried to summon images of vindictive retaliation if he were wrong about her. But grief complicated the images and wiped away his satisfaction. If he took revenge it wouldn't ease his gut-wrenching sorrow.

A rustling sound made his stiff fingers fumble for the shotgun. He squinted upward and aimed the gun as best he could. A huge, darkly furred shape appeared at the edge of the hole and peered down at him. Oh, hell. A bigfoot.

But Dinah halted beside the bigfoot and fell to her hands and knees. "How are you?" she called frantically.

A thrill sleeted through Rucker's body. She hadn't deserted him, even when she easily could have. Stunned, he only stared up at her in confusion and wonder.

"Oh, no! He's half-conscious," she cried.

Rucker blinked quickly and shook his head. His voice came out as a hoarse rasp. "I'm fine. But room service sucks." She sagged with relief. The thing beside her made an amused sound and moved out of his range of vision. "What was *that*?" Rucker asked.

"A mountain man. Drake Lancaster. We crossed paths, and he offered to help."

A thick rope tumbled into the hole. Rucker tied it to one of the timbers. Drake Lancaster's shaggy head poked over the edge of the hole again. "Good." He wound his end of the rope around hands the size of small platters and began to pull. A timber that must easily weigh three hundred pounds creaked, swayed, and rose slowly in the air.

Dinah continued to kneel beside the hole. Rucker caught her gaze, and she extended a hand even though she couldn't reach him. The gesture contained desperate concern and reassurance.

"Believe in me now," she urged him. "Believe."

Rucker never took his eyes from her. The warmth and hope that swelled inside his chest drove away his chills. She cared about him. Regardless of her vague and unsavory reasons for leaving him, she still cared about him. And if he was a fool for believing that, then so be it.

Drake Lancaster was the stuff of legends or nightmares, Dinah thought. He had a dangerous aura about him, the same aura she always sensed around Valdivia. Whether he measured honor by Valdivia's brutal standards she had no way of knowing, but it didn't matter.

He must be seven feet tall. His effect was accented by coal black hair and the long beard. Obsidian eyes glittered with intelligence from the background of what little she could see of his rugged face.

Now he stopped at the crest of a hill, and his brown greatcoat flapped back to reveal a heavy pistol strapped low on the leg of corduroy trousers. The handle of an enormous knife protruded from a sheath stuck in his belt. Lancaster pointed across a valley to several quaint log cabins that could be seen through the still leafless forest.

"There. Tom Beecher's rental place. Closed for a couple of weeks while Tom's on vacation, but the water pipes haven't been drained and the gas and electricity are on. Break the lock on the big cabin to your far right—that's Tom's personal cabin—and you'll find whatever supplies you need for the night. I'll tell him who broke in, and why."

Dinah looked at Rucker, who shared her expression

of weary curiosity. His clothes were filthy and damp. His legs were unsteady, and he leaned on Lancaster's walking staff. His determination to make the hour-long trek from the collapsed mine to this spot brought tears to her eyes. She held his elbow, trying in vain to help support him.

"Lancaster, you don't care where we're from or where we're goin'," Rucker noted grimly. "Why?"

The great, shaggy head turned toward them slowly. The look he gave Rucker would have cowed most men. Dinah watched her husband straighten subtly, his eyes unyielding. Dinah drew a soft breath of pride.

Drake Lancaster assessed him for a moment, then abruptly smiled. He held out a huge hand. A look of kindred respect crossed Rucker's face. His mouth crooked up at one corner as he shook the giant's hand.

"None of my business," Lancaster finally answered. "You don't ask me questions, I don't ask you questions." His gaze swiveled to Dinah. "He was worth saving," Lancaster noted.

"I know. Thank you." She was spurred by a feeling that there was a great deal more to Drake Lancaster than either she or Rucker suspected. He looked like a man unaccustomed to comfort or gratitude. Dinah kissed her fingertips, then reached up and touched them to his angular cheekbone. "Thank you again."

His dark eyes softened a little. He looked at Rucker. "You're lucky."

Dinah dropped her gaze and waited for Rucker's response.

"I know," he answered.

Lancaster half-bowed in a way that reminded her of some old-world gallant. Then he strode off without a backward glance. They stood for a moment, watching him until he disappeared in the snow-frosted woodland.

"Someone is looking out for us," Rucker commented.

Dinah pointed toward heaven. "You mean . . ."

"I hope that's what I mean. It just seems odd, that

human tank appearin' all of sudden when we needed him."

Dinah touched his cheek tenderly. His face was sallow with fatigue, and she suspected that she looked just as tired. "We deserve a little luck. That's all it was."

He mused over that idea for a moment then nodded. "You're right."

Dinah gestured toward the cabins. "Let's go. Lean on me and think of good things. A real bed. Food. We'll finally get a decent amount of sleep. Then onward to the highway at daybreak."

His undaunted green eyes burned into her with a hungry, primitive look that made her breath pull short. They had exposed too many raw emotions over the past two days to hide behind niceties now.

"We belong in that bed together," he told her.

While her heart thudded wildly, she gave him a jaunty look. "I'd planned on it."

The blue tinge to his mouth frightened her, and she knew that he needed warmth and food to fight the effects of the mine shaft.

"Damned legs," he grumbled, as she helped him to a chair by the cabin's hearth.

"They would have to be attached to you," she teased gently.

She and Rucker studied the rental cabin they'd selected for the night. It was a one-room dwelling, much smaller than the owner's cabin where they'd gathered canned food and necessities such as matches.

The furnishings were cheap but comfortable—an upholstered couch and chair that had probably seen better days in some family's den, a kitchenette with old white appliances, a tiny bathroom with a shower and tub unit made of molded plastic.

But the atmosphere was cosy, with a high-beamed ceiling, a stone fireplace, and a rough-wood floor covered in thick rugs. Dinah turned on the water heater first, then the space heater. Its red coils began to emit delicious heat. She adjusted the cabin's wall lamps so that their light was low and soothing.

Then she knelt by Rucker, who was rubbing his long legs from thighs to calves in an attempt to restore sensation. "Let me do that."

He took her hands in his. "Sssh. You're just as worn out as I am." The affection that flared between them suddenly made the cabin seem very warm. He leaned forward and brushed a kiss across her parted lips. "Forgive me for doubtin' you today. Forgive me."

Dinah rested her forehead against his and gloried in the sensations his firm mouth had aroused. "My darling, I know that you still have lots of reasons to distrust me. But just for a little while, can we pretend that everything's all right?"

"I'll try," he whispered.

Her throat burning, she rose awkwardly and stroked a gentle hand across his dirty cheek.

"I'll run the tub full of hot water, and you can soak."

Without waiting for his response she hurried to the bathroom. When heated water was hissing into the tub, she came back and found Rucker sitting cross-legged in front of the fire grate. As she watched, he coaxed a growing flame under a pile of kindling.

"My very own Boy Scout," she murmured as she handed him wood from a stack by the hearth.

"Wanta cross the street?"

"Hah. I'd be happy to find the energy to open two cans of beef stew."

"Forget the stew. Get that bottle of bourbon."

"A provocative notion, monsieur."

"Mon-sewer. I love it when you call me by my French name."

Laughing from nerves and fatigue and a giddy feeling she didn't need to examine too closely, Dinah brought him the half-empty bottle they'd found in the owner's cabin. She sat beside him on the hearth and gratefully absorbed the fire's heat.

He opened the bottle and looked at her speculatively. "What, no glasses? Is my little debutante going gauche on me?"

"Be quiet and let me have a swig."

They traded the bottle twice. Her two swallows of liquor hit her with intense effect. She leaned forward and mashed her face into Rucker's shoulder.

"Don't drool," he joked tenderly.

"Need food. Need sleep. Need you."

His voice was throaty. "You got it."

She drew back and tugged forcefully at his earlobe. "You're cold. Come take a bath."

"Yes, nurse."

He set the bourbon bottle on the hearth. She helped him to his feet and they went to the bathroom. Steam had already misted the tiny mirror over the sink, and the tub was about to overflow. Rucker bent over awkwardly and switched the water off.

Dinah shut the door, closing them inside the small room together.

He turned to gaze at her under arched brows. She looked up at him with wobbly reserve. "I'll help you undress," she announced.

"That's not a professional gleam in your eye, nurse."

"Sssh."

Her scent, her hands, her voice, and the loving fire in her eyes kept him mesmerized as she unfastened his clothes. Whatever happened beyond tonight, whatever secrets unfolded later, they were together now and he wanted nothing more than to believe in her.

She removed his shirt and undershirt by slow degrees, her eyes following the movements of her hands. He carried a great deal of his weight in his shoulders and darkly haired chest. When he stood before her bare from the waist up, she bent and placed nuzzling kisses down the center of his chest.

"Dee," he whispered, as his hands rose to stroke the unheeded tangles of her hair. It lay in damp strands down her back.

She trailed her hands to his jeans and unfastened them. "Sit on the edge of the tub," she commanded gently.

As he carefully lowered his abused body to the tub's rim, she pulled his clothes to his thighs. The jutting welcome of his manhood made her look at him with a bittersweet gaze. "Even an ice-cold pit can't keep a good man down."

He shook his head. "The night I walked into that city council meetin' and first saw you, I knew you were special," he whispered hoarsely. "Nobody else could make me so crazy with heat and tenderness at the same time. It's still that way."

"You overwhelmed me so much that I nearly forgot to be afraid of you. The big, bad columnist had come to make fun of me and my town, but all I wanted to do was ravish him!"

His mouth quirked up wryly. "You resisted that urge, as I recall. Despite my best efforts. I thought I was slicker than a snake oil salesman until I fell in love with a cross between Scarlett O'Hara and Katherine Hepburn."

"I didn't resist for very long," she reminded him. "It was love at first sight."

Rucker touched her face reverently. "I knew that I'd die for you if you wanted me to."

She began to cry softly while she removed his boots and finished undressing him. He tried to caress her tear-streaked face, but she ducked her head. "I'll cry harder," she explained.

"Then climb in the tub with me. You might as well get the rest of you wet."

She gazed at him in amusement, and a flush of pleasure rose in her cheeks. "That would be wonderful."

"Undress for me." His voice was low, soothing.

"All right." She stood and pulled her sweater over her head. He watched her with a languorous, completely possessive gaze, as if she were removing erotic lingerie instead of damp, dirty clothes.

She stripped the rest of her clothes off and stood before him expectantly. Her knees almost refused to support her as she stepped to him and rested her arms on his shoulders.

With a gruff sigh he nestled his face between her breasts. Dinah arched her head back and moaned as he trailed kisses across her tender flesh. He paused over a nipple, and she could feel his ragged breath on the ruddy, swollen peak.

"Are you in pain from havin' so much milk?" he asked.

"A little. But put your mouth on me anyway. Please."

His lips surrounded the taut nipple and sucked carefully. Her whole body sagged with incredible pleasure that was almost too exquisite to bear. When he moved to the other breast, he put his hand on the abandoned one and gently rolled the nipple between his thumb and forefinger.

Soon his fingers were covered with milk. They both looked at the evidence that they had created a baby. As swiftly as a shadow moving across the sun, the mood darkened.

"You need to be nursed," he noted. His tone became troubled. "Who's feedin' Katie right now?"

"Someone I trust. She's all right. I promise, my darling. She's all right. I'm not going to let anything happen to her." Dinah spoke past the choked tears in her throat. "Help me take care of the milk. Help me with your hands."

He settled in the tub and guided her down in front of him so that her back was nestled against his chest. They both sighed as the hot water cupped their bodies. "How should I touch you?" he whispered. His mustache tickled her ear.

"Like this." She guided his hands over her breasts until he could coax the milk without her assistance.

"Lean your head back on my shoulder and shut your eyes," he instructed. "You've been through so much hell lately. Just relax."

Following his suggestion was blissful.

Rucker sighed happily and circled her ear with the tip of his tongue. "The spirit's willin', but the body says, 'When pigs fly.' "

"Oh, please, no mention of pigs."

He hugged her tightly. "My brave girl. My sweet, brave girl."

She turned her face toward the crook of his neck and quivered as his hands moved again to her tingling breasts. "You're healing me with your touch," she said groggily. "You always could."

"Take a nap, ladybug. I'll sit here awhile and hold you and thaw out. Go to sleep."

"But you're so tired. You need—"

"I need to hold you." His voice nearly broke. "I've needed that so many times since you've been gone. Sssh. Sleep."

He began to hum an old gospel tune in her ear, his voice vibrating like a low-pitched tuning fork. A sweet darkness floated over her.

She was amazed when she woke up in the big bed that faced the fireplace. The cabin was shadowy and darkness pressed against the small, high windows. After a startled moment her exhausted body relaxed again, too tempted by the heat and softness that surrounded it.

The spicy-meat aroma of beef stew reached her nose and made her stomach rumble with need. Dinah blinked languidly and forced her eyes to focus.

What she saw made her smile. Rucker stood at the stove, his back to her. He wore nothing but his heavy blue hunter's coat, and it barely covered his muscular rump. She giggled, recalling his colorful and often vain descriptions of his physique. There was nothing shy about the way he displayed his body and used it to give her pleasure.

He heard her muffled laughter and turned around. The coat was open down the front, revealing a narrow but fascinating swath of hair, navel, and relaxed masculine attributes. When she pulled the covers up to her nose and batted her eyelashes in mock coyness, he grinned.

"What's it to you?" he demanded.

"You're wonderfully indecent, sir." He came to the bed and sat down beside her. She put her hands under his coat and burrowed her fingers in his chest hair. "I don't recall a thing after I went to sleep in the tub with you humming in my ear."

"I had a helluva time dryin' you off. You flopped over my arm like overcooked spaghetti."

"Why didn't you wake me up?"

"I like overcooked spaghetti."

She cupped her hands over his thighs and rubbed small circles. "Do your legs feel better?"

"Pretty much." His eyes gleamed in response to her touch. "Stop that. It's dinnertime."

"Food!" She started to push the covers down.

He halted her with a gentle hand. "Dinner in bed."

"Only if you're with me."

He smiled sardonically. "Did I dress to sit at the table?"

A minute later he brought two huge bowls of stew to the bed with hot biscuits propped on the rims. Dinah pulled herself upright and smiled incredulously. "Are these homemade McClure biscuits?"

He balanced both bowls on her outstretched legs and bowed low. "Hell yes, ma'am."

"Oh, how I've missed them."

Chuckling, he removed his coat, got in bed beside

her and took his bowl of stew. When his large, strong body nestled against hers she grew quiet. The contact subdued him as well. They looked at each other pensively.

He raised a spoonful of food and fed her, his eyes watching every movement her lips made. She lifted her spoon to his mouth, and when he swallowed the hot stew she bent toward him and kissed the movements of his throat.

They ate the rest of their dinner in that manner, without speaking more than a word or two. When they finished she carried their bowls to the kitchen. Dinah brought back a small glass filled with bourbon. She settled under the covers and took a swallow, then handed the rest to him.

"You always know what I want," he murmured. He tossed the liquor down his throat and set the glass aside.

She nodded, her body tingling with an almost frightening sense of anticipation. They had been apart so long, and she wanted him so badly, that she felt awkward. "Do you know what I want?" she whispered.

His barely perceptible nod combined with the searing sensuality in his eyes. Her blood sizzled; her skin was alert to every sensation. He guided her onto her back and pulled the covers away from her heated body.

His tongue drew a line of fire down the center of her stomach. When she moaned with joy he pressed his hand between her legs and made her body shift languidly.

He brought his mouth to each of her nipples and licked them. Dinah lay quietly, her palms turned upward beside her, her body and mind at ease for the first time in almost a year. He was her dearest friend, her lover, her husband, the father of the most wonderful child in the world. And one day, when he understood why she'd left him, life would be as perfect as before.

Sucking her skin lightly, he moved down her torso. His lips feathered over her stomach and his tongue traced patterns around her navel. His index finger probed the dampness between her legs and eased inside. When she gasped, he withdrew quickly. "Is something different now?"

Her voice was thick with passion and eager to reassure him. "No. *No*. It's just that I've spent so much time imagining how your touch would feel that I almost went over the edge."

His rough inhalation told her how powerfully those words affected him. He caressed her carefully, teasing her without repeating the earlier intimacy.

"You're very tight," he murmured. "Even after having a baby. Did you heal all right?"

"I think so. I feel fine."

"You feel fantastic." He moved up to her mouth and took it gently, exploring her lips and tongue with slow, thorough intent. She returned the exploration, and small cries echoed in the back of her throat as she thrilled to his taste and texture.

"I can tell that you never stopped wanting me," he whispered. "Nobody else has made love to you."

Her eyes snapped open and her body stiffened. She stared up into his large, expressive eyes and saw the harshness that tinged their green depths. Dinah felt the blood drain from her face. Now she understood. "You aren't loving me," she rasped. "You're testing me."

He nodded, and taut determination merged with the languorous desire on his face. "I'm doing both."

She inhaled raggedly. "I thought we had a truce."

"As long as you keep secrets about the past ten months, our truce is shaky at best."

She grasped his face between trembling hands. "Don't make a mockery of what I feel for you."

He laughed curtly and her blood chilled. She'd never thought him capable of such a sad sound.

"Look who's talkin'," he retorted.

"I *love* you."

A victorious glint appeared in his eyes. "Then don't

question my reasons for touchin' you. After what you've done to me, you ask for too much."

She felt her happiness crumbling. Dinah tried to pull him on top of her. "Just finish it. No more preliminaries. Come here. Maybe we can't hope for anything tender right now."

He grasped her hands and pressed them down on the bed. His eyes gleamed angrily. "Oh, no, you can't put that kind of wall around yourself. Lay back and close your eyes."

Without waiting to see her reaction he slid down her body and began to kiss her inner thighs. Dinah tried to close her legs; he roughly pushed them apart.

"I thought you were beginning to relax—to trust me," she protested tearfully.

"I trust you to tell me the truth eventually. I believe that you never stopped lovin' me, and I'm prayin' that I'll be able to live with the reasons why you left me. But right now I only know one way to prove that you're still mine."

"I don't want you to manipulate my body just to show me that you can."

She struggled to roll away from him, but he clamped an arm over her midsection. His voice dropped to a low, harsh level. "I told you that I can be cruel. Now lie still and take it."

He kept his arm over her and used his other hand to keep her legs spread. Dinah clenched her fists and stared at the ceiling. He lowered his head and began to torture her slowly and sweetly with his tongue. The contrast between his ugly words and his caring attention almost tore her defenses apart.

"You're movin'," he whispered smugly. "I can feel you pushing against my mouth."

"Physical stimulation is no mystery."

"You sound like a medical book. So logical. Let's see what's logical about this."

Months of loneliness and years of love were against

her in the battle to resist. She pressed her hips into the mattress to subdue her body's traitorous need to rise under his skilled mouth.

Even so she quivered and felt silky feminine moisture bathe the insides of her thighs. Rucker chuckled harshly and intensified his efforts, licking her sensitive skin as if she were covered in sweet syrup. When he tugged gently at the center of her aching flesh she cried out and sank her hands into his hair.

"Stop. Please. Don't use me this way."

"You told me I could use you anyway I wanted," he reminded her tersely. "As long as I helped you do your job. Did you think good ol' kind Rucker wouldn't take advantage of the offer? I'm not very kind anymore."

"Yes, you are," she answered brokenly. "And you don't really want to do this—"

"Stop talkin'!" A tremor ran through the hand that pushed at her thigh. His voice dropped to a strained whisper. "When I get through with you tonight you'll wonder why in hell you ever left my bed."

Dinah gasped silently at his words and their undertone of sorrow. Now she understood part of his anguish, and tenderness burst inside her. He feared that he hadn't been good enough in bed. Her chest constricted with mute sympathy.

Her legs relaxed bonelessly under his grip. This time when he delved into her she allowed the sensation to make her writhe. He pressed downward, forcing her to be still, making gruff sounds of satisfaction at her desperate attempts to seek more pleasure.

Rucker began to stroke her intimately with his hand again, teasing, circling. He groaned softly at her wild response. Her heels dug into the mattress and she tugged at his hair, almost fighting him because he held her down.

He doubled his efforts and a long, wailing sound of ecstasy tore from her throat while she raked her hands across his shoulders. Shudders of release cascaded through her until she could do little more than whip her head from side to side on the pillow and struggle weakly against the unceasing bondage of his arm.

He didn't stop until she was limp and panting. Then he straddled her and gathered her in both arms. Dinah looked up through a mindless haze of emotion and saw the heavy-lidded desire of a man who had been pushed past his limit. He raised her upper body off the bed so that she hung in his embrace with her head tilted back.

"Take it," he ordered.

His mouth, wet from her body, came down on hers desperately. Dinah draped her arms around his neck and reveled in the erotic savagery of his tongue. He kissed her with a plunging invasion that continued until she could barely breathe.

She twisted away, gasping, only to hear him make a menacing but surprisingly gentle sound. He caught her mouth again. This time he lowered her to the bed and quickly stretched out on top of her, his hips sinking between her thighs and angling them even farther apart. His hot, rigid male flesh was ready to enter her whenever he chose.

With a quick jerk of her head she pulled away from his kiss and looked up at him. He grabbed her head between his hands, then bent to taste her mouth again. Dinah managed to insert a hand between them and press it against his lips. He made a gruff sound of reproach.

"No more anger," she ordered in a soft, soothing tone. "I'm yours. I always have been and I always will be. When I left, it had nothing to do with not loving you. You gave me everything I needed, and I never looked for anyone else. I love you dearly. One day you'll believe that again. I promise."

He gazed at her with rising torment, then shut his eyes against emotions that made him quiver. Tears slid from under his dark auburn lashes. Dinah whimpered, then drew him to her and kissed them away. She pulled his head beside hers so that she could whisper in his ear.

"Make love to me, my darling. Now." Her hips arched to meet his thrust. She held him possessively, wrapping her legs around him and murmuring endearments until her own pleasure became so intense that she dissolved again under his powerful movements.

In the midst of her joy he lifted his head and feathered kisses across her mouth. She caught his ragged moan and mingled her own with it. He arched over her in a last, splendid motion that drove the past away and let new beauty begin to heal them both.

Eight

He was half-awake and sweating. Past and present tangled in a vivid dream, confusing him. She was innocent. Hadn't he helped her prove that? Rucker frowned deeply in his near-sleep state. No, not this time. He'd helped her years ago, before their marriage.

In the dream he could see her plainly, her face wan, her shoulders drawn back in a desperate attempt to keep her pride.

"My father was, according to a great deal of evidence, a thief and a liar. Right before his death he was about to be indicted by a federal grand jury for embezzling, fraud, and money laundering involving twenty-five million dollars."

She took a deep breath. "And I was suspected of knowing all about his activities. And deliberately concealing them."

He tried to comfort her, to tell her the past didn't matter. Her deep torment bewildered him.

"I wasn't innocent," she explained bluntly, her face flushed with humiliation. "When investigators began to come to me on the side, asking questions, I lied like a good daughter. I knew my father was involved in something illegal. I tried to talk to him about it, but he kept assuring me that nothing was as it seemed. And I believed him. Ironic, that I thought he was so wonderful . . . and it was all a lie."

Her face paled as she spoke the words. Suddenly her head tilted back and she sank bonelessly toward the floor. Rucker caught her in his arms and carried her to his bed.

She looked up at him weakly but ignored his pleas to rest and be quiet. His stomach knotted as he studied the horror that clouded her delicate blue eyes.

"Rucker, the courts said that I aided a felon. I was sentenced to three years in prison." She seemed to be tearing the words from the center of her heart. "I served one year."

Dizzy, spinning grief swept over him and his eyes stung with tears. He turned away and clutched the edge of the bed.

"Rucker?" she questioned anxiously.

"Give me a second." He drew deep breaths, fighting despair and fury. *How could anyone put this sensitive, honorable woman in prison?*

"I've always been terrified that when I told you about prison . . . that you'd be ashamed of me." She caught a strangled sound in her throat. "Are you?"

"Ashamed?" Dear lord, she was worried that he'd reject her. *"No!"* Something broke inside him, destroying the restraint that had been hammered into him as a child. A man who couldn't cry for his woman's pain wasn't much of a man.

Tears slid slowly down his face as he bent over her and rested his head against her shoulder. "Damn the whole freakin' world for doin' that to you."

Dinah stroked his hair with worried hands. "I love you so much," she whispered, her voice hoarse with emotion. "Sssh. It was bearable. I went to California and stayed in a minimum security prison, a country club sort of place."

He knew that she was surprised and touched by his

tears. She put her arms around him tightly and tried to make a joke. "I met *so many* interesting politicians and business executives."

When he got himself under control, he promised her that everything would be all right. A gossip-hungry television reporter had dogged her for years, intent on learning her secrets. Fear of exposure was the reason she'd dropped out of the Miss America pageant.

She was innocent. Rucker helped her clear her name and her father's. Her father had been framed.

But now . . . memories swam together in Rucker's mind and troubled him. He had to believe in her, as he had then. *Trust her*, his instincts urged.

But what would happen if she were guilty of espionage? Suppose her work with Valdivia—whatever her idealistic reasons—sent her to prison again?

This time she'd end up in a federal penitentiary, not some candy-land facility for the rich and powerful. Rucker gritted his teeth and twisted groggily, flinging an arm out in rough protest.

Dinah's soft, sleepy cry of pain stabbed through the fog of fear. Her hand fumbled against his face, then stroked soothingly. Rucker gave a shuddering sigh and blinked his eyes open. The thick, warm darkness wrapped them in a secure cocoon.

"Bad dream?" she murmured.

"Yeah."

"Tell me?"

He shivered despite the heat their bodies generated under the covers. "Can't remember," Rucker lied.

"Sssh. It's all right." She ran her hands over his shoulders and lightly scratched his back. "Bad dreams don't mean anything now that we're together again."

He could barely see her, but he felt the reassurance in her tender voice and pliant, sweet-scented body. She lay on her side facing him, her legs entwined with his. Her nipples touched his chest every time she inhaled, and the sensation electrified him. He realized that he had never felt more alive.

Lost in the unreal darkness and erotic sensations, Rucker relaxed into her embrace. He slipped his arms around her and was rewarded by a slow, loving kiss on the mouth. Cupping her tightly against his torso, he opened his lips for her gently searching tongue.

His pain was bittersweet. Who knew what tomorrow held? They might not get another night together. He could hardly bear the thought that there might never be another night like this one, when emotion and desire charged them both so completely.

The earthy scent of sex, the quick, light sound of her breathing, the way her mouth worshiped his in the darkness. She gave him this moment fully, and he let himself become lost in it. She *had* to be innocent.

"How I love you," he whispered hoarsely, his breath mingling with hers. "I've never stopped."

After a stunned moment, she made a ragged sound of happiness. "I never thought I'd hear you say that again. And I thought I'd die if you didn't."

"Don't die." Emotion turned his voice into a low rumble. "What would I do without you?"

She whispered across his lips. "I'll never let you find out."

He arched against her warm stomach, and she curled her fingers over the lean power of his shoulders. With movements that were slow and taut with restrained desire, they began to make love.

The sensual journey of his hand down her side was enough to make her writhe, and he watched breathlessly. As his eyes adjusted to the darkness she became an erotic mixture of shadows that surrounded him with desire.

The mattress was thick and yielding beneath them; it invited the wanton struggle for pleasure, the spreading of her legs and the lowering of his body between them.

Rucker thrust into her quickly and moaned at the swift answering contractions of her muscles. His single, powerful motion took her over the brink. She clasped his hips and rose under him.

Breathing heavily, he withdrew. Dinah protested with a low, keening sound. Rucker kissed her forehead and whispered gruffly, "I want it to last a long time. I'm too sensitive this way."

He lay down behind her and cupped her rump to his stomach and thighs. She purred low in her throat when she sensed his plan. Rucker pulled her top leg over his and slipped into the welcoming sheath he had sampled before.

"Now we can go slow," he murmured against her ear. He arched against her in a careful rhythm. Rucker brushed his hand over her belly and felt the muscles quiver.

"Sweetheart. Sweetheart, I can't . . . go . . . slow," she said with apology. She dipped her head and her body tossed against his like a willow caught in a storm.

With a desperate groan he grasped her hips and jerked them snuggly to his movements. His back bowed as he slammed against her and lost the last shred of control.

Rucker's breath shattered against her neck and his fingers dug into her heated skin, drawing cries of delight from her. Their bodies relaxed together like two taut wires sagging when tension is suddenly removed.

She wound her fingers through his while he raised them to stroke one of her breasts. He cupped it protectively and rubbed his thumb over the milk-slicked nipple.

His contentment was almost palpable; her love a force that brought him peace. Without speaking another word they fell asleep again.

Dinah watched his brows arch in appreciation even though his eyes remained shut. Smiling tenderly, she bent over him and held the coffee cup closer to his nose. Experimentally she drew the cup to one side. After a second, he turned his head toward it. Dinah suppressed laughter and moved the cup in the opposite direction. Sniffing, he turned his head that way.

She pressed a hand to her mouth and sat back quickly before her silent chuckles made her slosh hot coffee on his face. His eyes opened groggily, and he squinted at her in the dawn light.

In the mornings his deep, sexy voice sounded like a freight train slowly coming to a stop. "You got three seconds . . . to make me forget . . . that I'm awake. You better put . . . that damned coffee cup down . . . and get under the covers, woman."

She shook her head. "We have to move on."

Rucker raised up on his elbows and cursed boisterously as cold air hit his exposed chest and shoulders. Then he scanned her neatly braided hair, striped pullover, and jeans. "You're already dressed!"

"I thought it'd be easier this way." She put out a hand and touched his cheek. "It was incredibly tempting to stay in bed with you, but we have too much to do."

He sighed anxiously then nodded, thinking of the daughter he had yet to see. "If Lancaster was right, the road's not far from here."

"If we can just catch a ride, we'll be fine. Honey, I think you'll have to leave your shotgun behind. Who's going to give a ride to a pair of armed hitchhikers?"

"Damn. All right. What's for breakfast?"

"Cold biscuits and bologna."

He groaned. "Now *that* makes me want to get out of bed. I'm cold. Where are my clean clothes? Why didn't you turn up the heat?"

Dinah eyed him drolly. "I'd forgotten how much you remind me of Oscar the Grouch in the morning."

He swiped the cup of coffee into one large hand and drew her to him for a long kiss. She put her arms around his naked back and clung to him. Slowly he rested his cheek on her hair.

A pensive silence dropped over them. Underneath the teasing they were both very worried about the day ahead.

"Roll up your jeans and show an ankle. That always works in the movies."

"I'm wearing white athletic socks and running shoes. The effect wouldn't be terribly sexy, Rucker."

"I could stick out *my* leg."

"We don't want to attract female bears."

They stood close together for shelter against the biting wind. Snow gusted off the sagging branches of the pine trees that lined the road on both sides. Around a distant curve came a van.

"I didn't win all those beauty pageants without good reason," Dinah muttered. She put on her best smile, stuck her thumb out jauntily, and pressed her other hand to her heart in a gesture of sincere supplication. To Rucker she instructed, "Try to look all-American."

"If I had my shotgun I could do a Rambo impression. We'd get a ride for sure."

The van whizzed past without slowing. Its wheels slung melted snow at them. Dinah stumbled back and felt Rucker's broad hand catch her elbow.

"Son of a . . . that makes five times," he growled. "What happened to southern hospitality?"

Dinah patted his shoulder. "We better start walking, Rambo."

"Yo. How much further do we have to go? You told me yesterday, but I forgot."

"A little over an hour, if we had wheels."

"In feet time, that's two days."

She looked up at him worriedly. "I don't have two days. I have to start back south by tonight."

"We don't have two days. We have to start back south by tonight. Wherever you go, I go. Don't forget it."

Dinah nodded, smiling up at him. "I won't." An ugly sense of guilt curled around her rib cage, and she winced inwardly at the knowledge that she would have to sneak away from him somehow. She'd risk his fury before she'd risk his life.

As if reading her mind, he said in a warning drawl, "Dee."

She carefully formed a nonchalant expression. "What?"

"Promise me that you won't run when my back is turned. I'll never forgive you if you do."

Her breath stalled in her throat. The deadly intensity in his eyes and voice told her that he meant what he said. But of course he'd forgive her once he knew the truth about her situation—if she could prove it to him. She was banking on that desperate hope.

He wore no gloves, and his big, rawboned hands were chapped with the cold. She lifted them to her lips and kissed each palm tenderly, then looked up at him with all the sincerity she could muster. "I promise."

Slowly his mouth slid into a relieved smile and his eyes softened with apology for his tough words. "Let's start walkin'."

She trudged beside him down the road, her head bent and her hands curled under her poncho. It occurred to her that her body language practically shouted deception and guilt. Dinah snapped her head up and glanced at Rucker. He hadn't noticed, thankfully.

Dinah's heart began to patter raggedly. The new bonds they had formed last night were strong, but could they survive?

She had no time for brooding. They heard the whoosh of car tires coming up behind them. Dinah halted and watched as Rucker raised his hand to the driver of a paneled station wagon with darkly tinted windows.

The car continued past, drawing an icy gust of air

behind it. "Aw, your mother kisses gorillas," Rucker called. "Ugly gorillas."

"You're very immature, but I adore you."

They smiled wearily at each other. The sound of rubber screeching on wet pavement made them look back at the station wagon. It slid to a stop. The driver began to back up, zigzagging across the lane in haste.

Dinah blanched. "If there's a great big guy with a bad temper behind the wheel I think you'd better explain that your mother kisses gorillas too."

"Let's move off the road," Rucker ordered. "This jackass may be drunk."

He tossed their bags into a ditch, then grabbed her arm. They sloshed through snowy weeds to a safe spot. Wide-eyed, Dinah peered into the station wagon as it careened to a stop in front of them. The driver crawled across the front seat and shoved the passenger door open. Kneeling in the doorway, she stared at Dinah and clasped both hands to her mouth in tearful disbelief.

Dinah's mouth went dry and shock poured through her veins. "Anna!"

Dr. Anna Scarborough was still a cranky old broad, Rucker thought. His gentlemanly soft spot for women of all ages continued to fail him where she was concerned.

"I can't believe you brought *him* along," Anna announced as soon as he settled into the backseat. "This is no time for macho redneck interference."

"I like you too," Rucker said dryly.

"This is no time for bickering," Dinah said in an authoritative voice from the front seat beside the doctor. Her tone silenced them both.

Anna threw the car into drive and guided it up the road with a white-knuckled grip on the wheel. Rucker smiled grimly at her discomfort over his presence.

Her posture looked rigid inside serviceable leather shoes, loose gray trousers, and a thick flannel shirt.

She wore an oversize man's coat of brown cloth. Her mouth was clamped into a thin line and the floppy coat couldn't hide the angry set of her shoulders. Her short gray hair was disheveled, but that was its natural state back when they were neighbors in Mount Pleasant, Rucker recalled.

Anna wasn't one to care for appearances. In fact, she was damned eccentric, the epitome of the reclusive scientist.

For one thing, she raised exotic butterflies. For another, she named them. Spot. Pearl. Fred.

Her sharp brown gaze darted to the rearview mirror and glared at him. Her animosity was fierce, which didn't surprise him. Back in Mount Pleasant they'd shared a polite but unfriendly relationship.

But he hadn't minded that Dinah liked the old doctor. It amused him to listen to their skillful, complicated debates, and he loved to ruffle the doctor's feathers by playing devil's advocate. Dinah had enjoyed Anna's intellectual companionship even though the two of them disagreed on everything from art to world politics.

Rucker frowned. At least, they had seemed to disagree.

"What the hell kind of crazy scheme have you got my wife involved in?" he demanded tersely.

The doctor bristled. Dinah held up both hands in a peacemaking gesture. "Anna's not responsible for any of this."

Anna nearly hissed at Rucker. "Simple-minded patriotism is all you understand. Unlike life in your books, the real world is neither all black nor all white."

"Then describe the shades of gray," Rucker said between clenched teeth. "I want to know what business you and Dinah have with a Russian agent in South America."

Anna glanced frantically at Dinah. "Do you want to jeopardize *everything*? Why is he involved? Why?"

"Valdivia deserted me—he was being chased by U.S.

agents. I had to go on alone, without money, without anything. Rucker was the only person I could turn to."

"You could have called me!"

"Anna, our government is closing in on Valdivia. I was afraid you'd been discovered, that perhaps your phone was tapped."

After a moment, Anna sighed in disgruntled agreement. "How much does he know?" She jerked her head toward Rucker.

"Virtually nothing. He doesn't know about your work, or why I'm here, or what's happened over these past months. I figured that neither side could hurt him if he knew nothing."

"Valdivia won't see it that way."

"Yes, he will. He needs my cooperation too much. Until this last mission, I was the only person who could work for him in the U.S. without suspicion. I'm still the safest bet he has."

Rucker gripped the back of Dinah's car seat and spoke roughly. "You're through with this crap. We're goin' to South America and get our daughter, and I'm gonna hire a team of lawyers to keep you out of prison. You are *through* playin' spy. I know you must have good reasons for doin' it, but—"

Anna yelped. "He's going to Surador with you?"

Dinah fumbled with the edge of her poncho and looked away. "Yes. I'll explain later." Rucker's protectiveness made her eyes burn with bittersweet tears. He was willing to sacrifice everything for her even though he thought she was guilty of espionage against their country. For a deeply honorable man like Rucker, that decision must have been torture.

Anna's voice was cutting. "You seem to forget that I have as much at stake in this mission as you do. You're being selfish to take risks."

Rucker interjected sharply, "You don't have a daughter in Surador."

The aging scientist laughed bitterly, but her lower lip trembled. "I most certainly do, you idiot."

Rucker caught Dinah's cautious expression. She grasped Anna's arm and warned, "That's enough. He doesn't need to know."

Rucker sank back on the seat, frowning. He had hoped that this mess would begin to make sense once they reached their destination. But Dinah had an ally in crime now, and he felt even more isolated.

Anna Scarborough's house, like its owner, was unique and bizarre. It rose out of the side of a mountain like some sort of unnatural growth, a strange medieval design set in stone and log. It might have been the backwoods castle of a minor fiefdom run by a sorcerer.

The sorcerer stirred a banked fire in a massive stone fireplace. "Make yourself at home," she snapped, and waved a hand toward a heavy, leather-upholstered couch. "I'll bring herbal tea." She bustled out of the room.

"I'd need a suit of armor and a lobotomy to feel at home here," Rucker muttered under his breath.

Dinah pushed him down on the couch. "Don't antagonize her. Please."

He clenched his fists. "Back in Mount Pleasant she was a fascinatin' old radical who loved a good debate. I admired that about her. But now she's turned vicious. How in hell did you get involved with her?"

Dinah stroked his hair gently. "I can't tell you that right now. Let's just say that fate threw us together."

"What did she mean about havin' a daughter?" He could see that Dinah was debating the wisdom of telling him more. "At least tell me that," he urged her.

She trembled. "All right. Anna's daughter also has a doctorate in biology. Sara is about thirty years old. She's doing research in Surador's Amazon region."

"So what does she have to do with Valdivia?"

Dinah shook her head sadly. Her hypnotic blue eyes begged him to stop. "No more."

"What's gonna happen to me if I learn more?"

Her answer was swift and grim. "Valdivia will find out and kill you."

Shaken, Rucker got up and paced, his strides long and powerful. "How can you be sure of that?"

Anna Scarborough's soft, cynical laugh interrupted them. She stood in the doorway, a copper teapot in one hand. Her dark eyes glittered at Rucker. "Because she's seen him kill a man in cold blood. He made her watch."

"Enough!" Dinah vaulted to her feet. She shuddered uncontrollably and hugged herself in an attempt to stop. Her teeth chattered even though her voice was firm. "I won't t—talk about that. It's taken me m—months to forget it. Rucker, please. It makes me sick to talk about it. All right?" She shook her head wildly. "No more. No—"

"Sssh, Dee. All right." Rucker took a step toward her, his face white as he scanned her broken expression. He held out both hands. "Come here," he whispered gruffly.

The distraught love in his voice sent her running into his arms. He held her in a tight embrace and she rested gratefully inside the circle of his strength.

Anna still observed them from the doorway. She sounded almost sympathetic as she said, "You two look ragged. I have a guest room where you can rest for a little while. I'll bring you the tea when it's ready."

"Thank you," Rucker told her sincerely.

Dinah frowned as they followed Anna down a winding hallway to a room full of ornate furniture and rich tapestries. She kept telling herself that there hadn't been a devious undertone in the doctor's voice.

Afternoon sunlight slanted through the bedroom's narrow stained-glass windows. Dinah woke slowly, curled against Rucker with her head on his shoulder. Emotional exhaustion had taken its toll on them both.

After drinking the tea Anna offered they had fallen asleep, fully dressed, on the canopied bed. Dinah looked at Rucker's peaceful face and felt a wave of devotion rise in her chest. The windows' soft pastel shadows fell across his features, making him seem unreal, like some gallant knight from another time.

"I love you, Sir Sleeping Knight," she whispered. Dinah kissed his forehead gently. "Wake up."

He was strangely still, and his skin felt a little too warm to her lips. A small trill of alarm ran through her. "Rucker?"

There was no response, not even the flicker of his eyelashes. She shook him a little. His breathing was very deep and even. It never changed. Her voice rose desperately. *"Rucker!"*

She knelt beside him and took him by the shoulders. This time she put all her strength into shaking his big body. He was completely limp.

Dizzy with fear, Dinah leaped off the bed and ran to the room's heavy wooden door. She hauled the massive door open and raced into the hallway, calling Anna's name.

"Right here."

Dinah whirled around. The grandmotherly scientist sat in a high-backed chair, her hands resting calmly on the lion heads carved into the arms. Dinah's stomach churned. Anna had been waiting. She had expected this.

"What did you do to him?" Dinah demanded furiously, her voice lethal.

"Nothing harmful. His tea was drugged. He'll sleep soundly for another ten hours or so and wake up with a nasty headache. I'll give you some money, my car, and the package to deliver to Valdivia. By the time Rucker wakes up, you'll be with Valdivia in New Orleans. It's the only way. You know that."

Dinah assessed her blankly for a moment. A grim sense of logic and duty finally reasserted itself. "You're right," she admitted in a dull voice.

"Hurry. Every minute counts. I've prepared everything for you to leave immediately."

Dinah started toward the bedroom, then halted, her hands clenching rhythmically by her sides. "Tell him that I had nothing to do with drugging him," she ordered. "Tell him that I'll be back with our daughter. And tell him that I love him. Swear that you will."

She whirled around and faced Anna fiercely. "Swear it," she repeated.

"I swear. He's a good man, and I understand why you love him." The gray head nodded majestically. "You know that I have honor. Now go."

Dinah staggered back into the bedroom and sat beside Rucker. Tears streamed down her cheeks. She spent several minutes caressing his face. She ran her hands over his body so that she could commit every inch of him to memory. From a chest at the end of the bed she got a light blanket and covered him with it.

Finally, she held his head gently and kissed him on the lips. "Believe in me, sweetheart. Believe. I love you."

She turned and ran from the room.

Anna took one last look at Rucker's sleeping form and shut the door to the bedroom. She'd explain what she could when he woke, just as she'd promised Dinah. He mustn't blame his wife.

Foolish man. But she had to give him credit for bravery. And he was certainly intelligent. He loved deeply and with great loyalty. All in all, she admired him. If this terrible situation weren't wearing on her nerves, she wouldn't have goaded him so badly.

The house was quiet. Evening was drawing around. Anna went into her laboratory and through it to the solarium where thousands of butterflies fluttered around her as if in greeting. She turned her face up to their feathery caresses and began to cry.

The shrill drone of her alarm system jerked her from the moment of weakness. Anna wiped her crinkled face and hurried through the house. She entered the medieval hall she called a living room and halted in shock.

A black-haired giant stood there, an automatic pistol hanging nonchalantly in his hand. Beside him stood a beautiful fair-haired man of only average height whose presence nevertheless seemed very overwhelming.

"Dr. Scarborough," Jeopard Surprise said with a cold smile, "you're under arrest."

Nine

The headache was like the one in the old commercial, where tiny hammers beat a catchy rhythm. His was an unceasing, thumping rumba.

Rucker woke with the heels of his hands pressed into his eye sockets. He put a hand out on the bedcovers, searching for Dinah. Her cool, loving touch was the only thing short of brain removal that might help him.

"Hurts like the devil, I bet. The side effect is usually like that."

"Move slow, Rucker. You'll be all right in a few minutes."

The unexpected male voices shocked him into awareness. He squinted in the dim light of a bedside lamp. Jeopard Surprise sat on the far corner of the bed, one arm resting on an updrawn knee. He was utterly sophisticated, yet casual. Redford playing Bond, Rucker thought woozily.

But the languid pose was so different from Jeopard's usual formality that Rucker sensed deception. Jeopard was deliberately trying to put him at ease, to reassure him. A huge, oddly familiar man lounged against one of the bedposts, looking equally nonchalant.

Pain knifed through Rucker's forehead when he sat up. He swayed, braced his arms beside him, and rasped, "What the hell is goin' on? Where's Dinah?"

The giant handed him a glass of water and two tablets. "She's all right. Take these and your head won't hurt quite as bad."

Rucker swallowed the painkillers and looked around groggily. Night had fallen outside the colorful windows. He raised his wrist and blinked at his watch with fierce determination. "It's three A.M."

"Congratulations. Most men who wake up from a heavy dose of narcotics can't remember their names for a while, much less tell time," Jeopard said pleasantly.

Rucker drew his knees up and leaned on them for support. He knew that this turn of events was disastrous, but his thoughts were too sluggish to figure out why. "Where's Dinah? What are you doin' here? Where's Anna Scarborough?"

Jeopard continued in the same cocktail-party voice. "Dr. Scarborough is under arrest. She's been taken away for questioning." He paused. "Dinah is on her way to meet Valdivia."

Rucker raised his head slowly. Jeopard's announcement cleared his pain as cleanly as if a scalpel had excised it. "No. I was supposed to go with her. We had an agreement."

Jeopard gave the news to him bluntly, without blinking. "I doubt she ever intended to keep it. Drugging you was the easiest way to solve the problem."

Rucker felt sick. Then his mouth curled in disgust. "She left me a note and you have it. Give it here."

"Rucker, there's no note. What would I gain by hiding it from you?"

Rucker jammed a hand through his hair. After a bitter moment his shoulders slumped. "All right. But my wife wouldn't dope me. She's not capable of that."

"I'm sorry, friend, but that's not the way it appears. We don't have the details because Dr. Scarborough is staging a silent protest. She refuses to say a word about *anything* she or Dinah did. But you've been drugged, and your wife's gone, and my men are following her. It's time for you to wake up—in more ways than one."

The implication washed over Rucker and a nauseating fist twisted in his stomach. He lurched up from the bed and staggered blindly toward the bathroom, clutching his midsection.

He refused to believe this. Fury supplanted shock. When he returned, bent halfway over, he jabbed a finger at Jeopard. "You cold bastard, you don't love anybody so I don't expect you to understand how my wife feels about me. Or how much I believe in her. Catching her and Valdivia is nothing but a damned job assignment to you."

Jeopard's lounging posture never changed, but his face tightened into a grim smile. "Oh? Valdivia killed my brother."

Rucker gazed at him in speechless astonishment. Kyle. Jeopard's brother. Millie's brother. Kyle had worked with Jeopard in Navy intelligence and later as a freelance government agent. Kyle was one of the most decent, likable men in the world.

"I thought he was on assignment somewhere in Asia," Rucker finally managed.

Jeopard shook his head. "Kyle was in Surador about three months ago, investigating Valdivia. He learned that Dinah was living at one of Valdivia's haciendas. Kyle smuggled a message to her and she offered to meet him. When she did, Valdivia got him."

Jeopard paused, as if taking a moment to carefully suppress his emotions. "My information is sketchy, but as best I've been able to learn, Valdivia put him in a sealed courtyard with a pack of rottweilers."

Rucker took a long breath. Dinah had watched a man die. Kyle Surprise. She was nervous around dogs now. He asked slowly, "Are you sayin' that Dinah deliberately helped Valdivia set Kyle up?"

"It looks that way." Jeopard was silent, as if a spell had just turned him into marble. "Everything I know about her is documented by indisputable evidence. Everything you know is based on what's she's told you over the past few days." He lifted his hands in a gesture of regret. "You got vague assurances from a woman who once spent a year in prison and is faced with the prospects of going there again if I catch her."

"Damn you." Rucker groaned in bitter protest to Jeopard's logic. He went to the bed and sank down weakly. Dinah was gone. She'd left him, tricked him, drugged him without the least hint of concern. Jeopard wasn't lying about that.

"I'm on your side," Jeopard told him finally, his voice strained. "I'm not the one you should hate. Try hating Valdivia."

"That's easy."

"My men should be arresting him in a few hours. As soon as Dinah leads them to him."

Rucker gasped for breath. The only pain inside him now was the pain of old wounds tearing open. Then bitterness seeped into the pain, fusing it into something unyielding and deadly. He had trusted her. Never again.

He rasped the words. "I have a daughter in Surador. At one of Valdivia's plantations, I think."

After a moment of stunned silence, Jeopard commented, "That's news to me. But it's possible."

"Anna Scarborough's daughter is workin' with Valdivia."

"We know. She's a loose end we don't intend to ignore."

Rucker looked at him sharply. "As in 'terminate with extreme prejudice?'"

"Relax, friend. I don't kill people. I meant that we have locals working to find her. We suspect that she's at one of Valdivia's haciendas. Possibly the same one as your daughter."

Rucker could think of little beyond his grief and

anger. His dazed vision settled on the man beside Jeopard. Above a now clean-shaven jaw, black eyes gazed back at him.

"Lancaster."

The dark head bowed slightly in acknowledgment. "I had to make certain you got out of the mine."

Rucker swiveled his gaze to Jeopard. "You tracked us all the way here. You let Dinah escape. She was right. I was carryin' a transmitter. How?"

Jeopard nodded toward Rucker's watch. "It was the only way I could find Dr. Scarborough."

"And now your men will just follow Dinah back to . . . to where?"

"New Orleans. She's probably there by now. As soon as she meets with Valdivia, we'll arrest them both. And take the package she was to deliver."

"What's in the package?"

"A herbicide that Valdivia's superiors are very interested in obtaining."

"What do the Russians want with a weed killer?"

Jeopard's voice was soft. "I think they want to destroy most of the plant life in the United States."

Rucker absorbed the information and felt his last bit of faith drain away. Dinah was party to an evil he could hardly fathom. She must have been desperate to do anything, to say anything that would keep him off the track.

Rucker didn't recognize his own voice. It was completely devoid of emotion. "So that's what Dr. Scarborough's been workin' on. She and her daughter."

"Looks that way. It has something to do with a virus carried by a certain species of South American butterfly. They concocted a synthetic form of the virus, at least a million times more potent than the original. Dinah is just their courier, if that makes you feel any better."

"Just the courier."

"Rucker?"

"Hmmm."

"We'll take you to see her tomorrow. She'll be under isolation and heavy security, but I can pull strings."

"I don't want to see her. I just want to get my daughter out of Surador."

"You're glassy eyed and upset. See how you feel in the morning."

"I'm not one damned bit upset." Rucker held out a hand. "Steady as a rock." He lay down, shut his eyes, and fumbled with the light blanket that had been covering him when he woke. How thoughtful. Dinah hadn't wanted him to catch a chill.

"Get out," he growled at Jeopard and Drake. "I need to think a while."

"All right. Good enough. We'll be around."

"Get out."

He heard the heavy thud of the door closing. Then he heard the creaking of a chair as someone settled into it. Rucker turned furious, dazed eyes toward a thronelike contraption in one corner. Drake Lancaster sat there, his hands crossed over his stomach, his legs stretched out in front of him.

"I said I need to think, dammit."

Lancaster nodded companionably to him. "I like to watch people think. But don't think too hard while you hold onto your blanket. You just ripped a big hole in it."

"The sun is hot these days. There are lots of reasons to watch the stars."

Her heart jumping, Dinah halted in the lobby of the New Orleans hotel and stared at the young woman who'd just spoken those words to her. The woman wore a sloppy brown dress suit. Her red hair spilled in fuzzy disarray to her shoulders. She carried a dingy leather purse and a handful of newspapers. Agents were hardly glamorous creatures.

Dinah inhaled sharply. "Astrology could be the answer to our questions."

Nodding and smiling, the young woman handed her a copy of the daily paper. "Enjoy." She left the lobby at a casual pace.

Dinah located the lobby restroom and hid in a stall. There she opened the newspaper and found the note she expected. Valdivia's dark, slanting script leaped out at her: *Danger. Change of plans. Meet me here.* He listed a street address and time.

Her head ached from lack of sleep and long hours of driving. Nervousness made her hands shake as she disposed of the note. It could mean only one thing. They were being followed.

Rucker had never seen Jeopard Surprise visibly angry. The fact that Jeopard was now pacing in front of Dr. Scarborough's fireplace meant that the phone call he'd just received had brought extremely bad news.

Drake lounged against a wall opposite the chair where Rucker sat. "Did somebody screw up in New Orleans?" he probed.

Jeopard nodded. "We lost them both. Valdivia met Dinah in an abandoned warehouse. The two of them slipped out a hidden exit. They've left the country by now. We'll pick the trail up in South America, but we won't have the jurisdiction to arrest either of them."

"Just find out where they're going," Rucker told him in a flat, unemotional voice. "And tell me."

Jeopard stopped pacing and gazed at him sardonically. "So you can go down there and get killed? Hell, no."

"I'm going after my daughter. I don't need your permission."

He watched Jeopard and Drake share a shrewd look. "You need our help, though," Jeopard remarked. "Unofficially, of course. Hmmm. A domestic dispute. An upset husband wants to bring his wife and child back to the States. He resorts to kidnapping. Understandable."

Rucker felt his teeth grinding at the inside of his cheek. "I don't want my wife back."

"Maybe not, but I have to insist. I want Sara Scarborough, too. Unfortunately, we can't kidnap Valdivia along with them—the extradition legalities would ruin us, since he's a Suradoran citizen. But bringing Dinah and Sara back is a good start."

Drake straightened and stretched languidly. "Give me a couple of days to get some surveillance reports on Valdivia's location. Then we can move in. How many men do you want?"

Jeopard smiled thinly. "Just the three of us. We're simply overworked businessmen taking a few days off to visit Surador with a friend."

If Drake felt astonished or worried, he hid it well, Rucker noted. The huge man merely shrugged. "A nice way to spend a vacation. I'll make the reservations." He arched a black brow wryly. "I suppose we're traveling tourist class?"

Jeopard bowed toward Rucker. "Certainly. Our friend is paying the expenses. Wouldn't want to take advantage of his hospitality."

Rucker shrugged. "We'll go first class. If you two are gonna risk your lives, the least I can do is make it pleasant."

"You'll be risking yours too," Jeopard reminded him.

Rucker looked at him wearily. "No problem. It's not much of a life anymore."

The hot, green smell of the jungle would always mean fear and captivity to Dinah. She shut her eyes and recoiled inwardly as Valdivia's armed driver opened the Mercedes's passenger door.

"Home sweet home," Valdivia murmured slyly, as he got out of the car. He turned, a tall, imposing figure in an exquisite dark suit, and offered his hand. "Come now, *querida*. You always look so unhappy when we return to my plantation. But you'll be with your daughter again, and I know you'll enjoy seeing Sara.

"You should go straight to your suite and rest. Your maid will run a cool bath for you. Then you and I will have a very pleasant dinner in my private courtyard."

Dinah let him help her from the car. She gazed up at the sprawling, white-washed hacienda surrounded by majestic trees. Despite its luxury and Spanish charm, it was a prison. Wrought-iron bars covered the windows of her suite.

"I don't have a maid," she retorted. "I have a guard."

Valdivia slipped an arm around her waist as they walked to an arched entranceway draped in flowering vines. Servants in brightly colored clothes bustled ahead of them. "It need not be that way," he insisted smoothly. "You and little Catalina could have a very fine life here. I have made offers—"

"My daughter's name is Katie. You have made a bargain. I expect you to keep it."

He sighed. "Allow me to examine the package from Dr. Scarborough, and then we'll talk."

"The project is over, Diego. You have what you want. Now you have to let us go. And Sara."

There was a harsh edge to his voice. "I will examine the package," he repeated. "This discussion is ended." He paused. "Tonight at dinner you'll wear the green dress with the emerald earrings. And wear your hair up." He stroked her waist through the blue linen of her suit. "You must tell me how you lost your sable coat. I want to know everything about your adventures."

Dinah stiffened miserably. She'd have to spend the rest of the afternoon concocting a plausible story that would exclude any mention of Rucker. The pain that ran through her at the memory of his drugged, helpless body made her stomach churn.

Believe, my darling. Believe.

• • •

Drake waved them to a stop. "We're almost there. Let's take a break and go over everything one more time."

Rucker ran a sweaty hand along the back of his neck then shrugged gear off his back. They'd spent hours in airplanes, then more in a rented truck, and now they'd hiked at least ten miles through a lush hell of jungle.

But fatigue was no match for the emotions that drove him. He stood with his legs braced apart, staring into the forest ahead of them. Valdivia's plantation was close.

He'd steal his wife and daughter from the bastard, even if his wife didn't want to be stolen. He'd take Katie to Mount Pleasant and together they'd create some semblance of a normal life. Dinah would go to prison, which was what she deserved.

Rucker forced himself to listen as Drake went over the layout of the hacienda one more time. They'd all three memorized it from surveillance reports provided by a local informant.

But he kept seeing Dinah's face and hearing her words from the past week. How could he have mistaken deception for devotion? How could he drag her back to the States and let strangers lock her away?

Damned fool, he called himself. *Don't think, just do it.*

He realized suddenly that Jeopard was speaking to him. Rucker turned toward him, frowning. "What? Say that again?"

Jeopard clasped his shoulder. His face was stern, but his voice held gentleness. "I said, Don't look in Dinah's eyes. It'll be easier that way."

Rucker felt as if he'd been punched in the stomach. He fought to subdue the emotions that suddenly wanted to take charge again. His jaw clenched, he finally managed to nod in agreement.

Don't think. Just take revenge.

• • •

"Katie. Oh, Katie Ann. Your father already loves you, even though he hasn't met you yet."

Dinah cradled their daughter's soft, small body to her shoulder and brushed a kiss across her forehead. She cherished these private times when she was allowed to sit alone with Katie in the walled garden behind the hacienda. Trees broke the tropical sun into harmless dapples. Here it was safe for Katie to wear nothing but a diaper.

Dinah stroked her fluffy hair. "Exactly the color of your father's," she crooned hoarsely, unable to hide the tearful undertone in her voice. Katie stirred. Her head wobbled up and Dinah studied the tiny frown between her eyebrows.

Dinah forced a reassuring smile. "Sweetheart, I didn't mean to upset you. There. That's it, close your eyes. That's my girl."

Moving slowly, Dinah put her down on a white blanket cushioned by the manicured lawn. Katie's lips moved with contented nursing motions. Her tiny hands curled and uncurled. Delicate auburn eyelashes fluttered against her cheeks.

Dinah swallowed a familiar knot of anxiety. She drew her knees up and rested her head on them, wrapping the skirt of her white, shirtwaist dress around her legs as she did. With one hand resting protectively on Katie's leg, she allowed herself to slip into a daydream.

When Valdivia let her leave, she'd take Katie straight to Mount Pleasant. Sara Scarborough would come with her. They'd explain everything to Rucker from start to finish and get Anna to add her part of the story.

When Rucker heard, how could he *not* believe them? The story was too incredible to be a lie. He'd help them defend themselves.

When the dust settled, she would surround herself with Rucker's love and together they'd erase the heartache of the past ten months. She imagined all the things she'd do for him, and all the wonderful things he'd do in return. They'd be homebodies, playing with Katie, reading aloud to each other, working in the yard, making love in their king-size bed. . . .

Sounds behind her made her grimace with dismay. Dinah raised her head and said in fluent Spanish, "Teodora, you promised me a full hour today. I have twenty minutes left."

A hot, strong hand clamped over her mouth. Dinah screamed uselessly against it. Other hands pulled her arms behind her and snapped cuffs on them. She tried to twist away, but the grip on her arms was unyielding.

Dinah darted a frantic gaze toward Katie, whose eyes had opened wide at the frightening sounds of struggle. The hand moved from Dinah's mouth but immediately a thick strip of adhesive tape took its place.

She writhed wildly, elbowing the hard, muscled body behind her so that its owner grunted with discomfort. She drummed the grass with her heels. Suddenly a powerful arm snaked around her waist, pulling her against a sweaty chest.

Dinah thought she must be losing her mind. Something in the scent and feel of the man was not only familiar, but reassuring. She made furious and despairing sounds that were muffled by the tape over her mouth. A thick mustache brushed her ear.

"Shut up and be still," an unmistakable voice whispered.

Shock brought dizzy pinpoints of light into her vision. She froze, breathing harshly. Oh, God, no. Rucker had somehow managed to follow her to this hellhole.

Dinah stared with dazed eyes as a gigantic man came around in front of her. He wore army fatigues and a deadly looking machine gun was slung over his back. His black hair was plastered to his head by sweat and his skin was ruddy from exertion, but his expression was utterly calm. He squatted beside her, grabbed her ankles, and cuffed them with bright silver links.

Confusion stabbed her. Why were they treating her like this? She tried to call out to Rucker but the words were muffled. He scooped Katie and the blanket into his hands. A second later he left her limited range of vision and she realized that he was walking away. Incredulous, Dinah shoved the giant with both feet.

He lost his balance, grunted in surprise, and fell out of his squat. Dinah rolled over on her stomach and watched anxiously as Rucker reached the garden's tall, white-washed wall. He wore the same kind of combat gear as the giant.

To her amazement, Jeopard Surprise was perched on top of the wall. Rucker handed Katie up to him. With the baby clasped in both arms, Jeopard dropped to the outside.

Massive hands slipped under Dinah's waist. She gasped as the giant picked her up and hung her face-down over his shoulder.

In less than a minute she found herself outside the garden wall. Her stomach muscles protested painfully as the giant carried her into the jungle behind Rucker and Jeopard.

When they were several hundred feet from the hacienda she heard Jeopard order softly, "Here."

She was lowered to the matted jungle floor. The giant rolled her onto her stomach and she awkwardly tried to keep her face out of the damp humus. Someone slipped a soft cloth beneath her head. Dinah rested her cheek against it and frowned in bewilderment as she realized that it was Katie's blanket and that the kindness came from Rucker.

Why didn't he just turn her loose? Did he think she'd run or scream?

"Drake and I'll be back soon with the other one," she heard Jeopard say. "Just keep Dinah still and quiet."

Drake? Dinah noted instantly. As in Drake Lancaster, the bearded mountain man? Rucker's deep voice interrupted her bewilderment. It held a coldness that stunned her.

"She won't be any trouble anymore. I'm only worried about my daughter." Dinah heard Katie's soft coo. Rucker spoke again, his voice softer. "But this little lady's a tough gal, I can tell already. She won't make a peep."

After the other two men departed, Dinah heard only her own harsh breathing and the tentative sounds of birds and insects that had been startled into silence by the human activity. Then there was the rustling movement of Rucker's army boots as he moved about. She heard him talking to Katie, but his voice was too low to understand.

Suddenly his laced boot came down inches from her face. He was standing over her, his feet braced apart. She could almost feel his gaze. Dinah braced her shoulder into the ground and tried to roll over. To her amazement, he put a foot on her back and held her still.

The careful force didn't hurt, but her emotional distress burst into anguish that made her groan with grief and frustration. Immediately he removed his foot and sat down beside her. He gripped her shoulder firmly.

"Don't move," he rasped in a low, fierce tone. "And get used to bein' a prisoner."

Understanding finally sank into her stunned thoughts. Just as he'd warned, he would never forgive her for leaving him, no matter what loving message Anna had passed along. Trembling with despair, she clenched her hands against the thick steel cuffs.

Abruptly Rucker reached for her right hand. "I kept warnin' you not to cross me. I told you that I'm capable of bein' cruel now." He pried the fingers open. "Valdivia outfits you pretty well," he noted, twisting the ring on her third finger. "Looks like a sapphire. You must have told him how much you like them."

He pulled the ring off. "Too bad." She sensed the

movement of his arm as he tossed the ring into the undergrowth. Next he removed the matching bracelet. "You won't need this anymore." She heard it strike the heavy frond of a plant nearby.

His fingers fumbled at her sapphire earring. It suffered the same fate as the other pieces of jewelry. "Now the other side." Lacing his fingers into her flowing hair, Rucker made her turn her head toward him.

From her awkward position she could see him by straining her side vision. Katie lay on his lap, gazing up at him raptly and without fear. Dinah blinked swiftly but couldn't control the burning in her eyes. Tears of bittersweet joy slipped across the bridge of her nose.

"Damn you, don't cry for sympathy," Rucker growled. He pulled the other earring off and threw it viciously. "What you feel doesn't make any difference to me. I won't take the tape off your mouth and risk havin' you scream for help."

Dinah choked back sobs, knowing that she would hardly be able to breathe if she gave into them with her mouth taped shut. She turned her face away from him once more.

"You had me hooked, lady," he told her in a flat tone. "I started trusting you again. Congratulations. But you made a mistake when you drugged me like some sort of animal you wanted tamed."

Anna hadn't given him the message. Dinah trembled in despair. Her throat strained with the need to explain to him. He couldn't be in any more danger than he was already. There was no more need for secrecy. If he'd only give her a chance, she'd tell him everything.

"Let's see what else Valdivia likes," Rucker said tautly. He repositioned himself by her legs. "An ankle chain, babe? That's tacky—not your style." He anchored several fingers under the slender thread of gold and broke it. He pulled one of the white flats from her feet. "Italian.

Very freakin' nice." He pulled the other shoe off and flung them both away.

"No hose. Well, it's so hot here, and I always said you have great legs." Dinah gave a muffled cry as Rucker flipped the long skirt of her dress up to her waist. She winced at his harsh intake of breath.

Valdivia had refused to let her have any panties. It was one of the more ridiculous ways in which he could taunt her for resisting his advances.

"Let's see the rest." This time Rucker's voice quivered with controlled rage. He flung her skirt back over her bare hips and grasped her by one arm. "Roll over."

Tugging her quickly, he turned her onto her back. His fingers grasped the top button at the V-necked bodice and tore it off. He roughly shoved the material aside. She wore an ugly nursing bra with wide shoulder straps.

"Hell. This must really put him off. I bet he can't wait until you get rid of it."

For the first time Rucker's eyes met hers. She looked at him with understanding and sadness. Her gentle gaze seemed to stun him; he cursed weakly and turned his head. "Jeopard warned me. He was right."

With a quick movement he rolled her onto her stomach again.

Dinah lay there in silent misery, and he shared it. Finally Katie made a series of soft, funny sounds. "Nobody can hurt you now, sweetpea," Rucker said, his voice low and gruff. "We're goin' home." His next words were meant for Dinah. "At least I feel sure that she's my daughter. She couldn't have gotten this color hair from Valdivia."

Dinah nodded stiffly. Her neck ached from the uncomfortable position and the small of her back felt as tight as a bow. Perspiration streamed down her sides. Her breasts hurt from being mashed against the ground.

Rucker must have sensed her discomfort. He grasped her shoulders and pulled her to a sitting position with her back to him. She twisted to look at him over her shoulder.

He was gazing at Katie. The baby flailed her arms and held one hand up, curling her fingers at him. He put his little finger within her reach and she wrapped her hand around the tip. He gently tickled her stomach. "What a smile," he whispered in a tormented voice.

Dinah sighed. Katie had *her* smile.

He looked up sharply and caught her watching them. His expression darkened. "Face the other way."

Wearily, she did so. He spoke again, his tone cold. "You won't get to see her grow up. You'll go to prison. You'll get old in prison. And all that time you'll be thinkin' about Katie, wonderin' how she is, what she's doing, what she looks like. She'll never think of you as her mother."

All of what he was saying was entirely possible. She and the Scarboroughs had no proof that they weren't willing participants in Valdivia's work. Dinah threw her head back and groaned against the binding tape.

"Good," Rucker said harshly. "I'm glad you're upset. I don't know how in the hell you can justify what you were doin' for Valdivia. A deadly herbicide—that's the sickest kind of war."

Before he could say anything else rain began to cascade down on them. The sky had been sunny minutes earlier, but unexpected downpours were a daily event in the Amazon. Even the huge trees above them offered little protection.

Katie let out a wail of pure distress. Rucker put her on the ground and lay down on his stomach with his torso braced over her as a shield. Still she cried, and her angry bawling resonated through the jungle.

Dinah looked around frantically, afraid that one of Valdivia's workers might be roaming within earshot. She lay down on her back and wormed her way under Rucker.

His eyes glittered with warning and he started to

protest. But when Dinah turned her face toward Katie's and rested her forehead against her cheek, the baby's wails subsided. Dinah felt one tiny hand grab a strand of her hair as if it were a pacifier.

Warm rain continued to pour down on them. Above her, Rucker was oblivious to it. Shocked by her actions to help him, he stared down at her and Katie, his eyes moving over the visible evidence of their loving bond. Dinah's eyes glistened like blue crystals, and the quiet plea he saw in them was too tormenting.

His hand shaking, he fumbled with the tape over her mouth.

Don't do it. Look away from her.

But she helped me—she knew I'd be in danger if somebody heard Katie crying.

Don't be stupid. It doesn't mean anything.

It has to.

He carefully pulled the tape away. Dinah drew several deep breaths and looked up at him with apparent adoration. "I can tell you everything now," she called against the loud background of pounding rain. "Whatever you want to know." As he gazed at her warily she laughed with joyful relief that bordered on crying. "My darling, I've waited for this moment for so long . . ."

"*Atención! Ya ha terminado!*"

Their world exploded in movement as Valdivia's men surrounded them.

Ten

His guards had discovered Jeopard and Drake just as they were carrying Sara Scarborough into the jungle, Dinah learned later. After capturing them, the guards began searching for her and Rucker.

"I kicked the blond guy in the groin and he barely flinched," Sara whispered as she and Dinah stood on the gallery that overlooked one of the hacienda's small courtyards. "If I'd known that he was here to rescue us, I would have wrapped myself around him like a hungry anaconda. But he and the other one caught me as I was coming out of the lab. No explanation. They just grabbed me."

Sara, whose small size made her look deceptively delicate, shook back a long mane of red hair and added, "Dinah, they might be worth something to Valdivia as hostages. He won't hurt them."

Dinah clasped trembling hands in front of her and glanced at the guards posted near them. "The way he didn't hurt Kyle?"

Sara started to say something else, but Valdivia strode onto the gallery, smiling wolfishly at them. Dressed in white tennis clothes he faked a wholesome appearance. He stopped by Sara and looked from her to Dinah.

"Some excitement, eh? I see you've both changed and cleaned up. Admirable, the way you've recuperated from such an ordeal."

He touched the sleeve of Sara's breezy red-print dress and waved an approving hand at Dinah's elegant blue silk. "We should have a lawn party."

Sara laughed sweetly. "You could chain Dinah and me to some croquet wickets and hit balls at us. Wouldn't that be fun?"

Valdivia flashed her a smiling, slit-eyed warning. "Possibly." His mocking eyes rose to Dinah's. "But I wouldn't want to provoke Dinah's husband. Anger makes him foolish."

Dinah suppressed a furious desire to put her hands around his throat. Her back rigid, she said softly, "My husband knows virtually nothing about you. He's no danger to you. What do you intend to do with him?"

"I'm not certain, *querida*. Let's have a closer look at our catch."

He leaned over an ornate white railing and motioned to a guard below. A door opened. Several armed men shoved Rucker, Jeopard, and Drake into the courtyard.

Dinah's knees went weak when she saw the stiff way they moved. She grasped the railing tightly. "You had them beaten, you bastard," she accused Valdivia in a low, dangerous voice.

Sara exclaimed hoarsely then adopted the poker face that had protected her all these months.

Valdivia laughed. "Not badly. Not so that it would show. I didn't want to upset you."

The three prisoners raised their eyes to the gallery. Dinah met Rucker's gaze and nearly sank to the gallery floor in horror. His eyes held physical pain and something much worse—fierce loathing.

Valdivia must have seen her hand flex as if to reach out to Rucker. "Don't, *querida*," he warned in a soft, lethal voice. "Play your part or he won't have any chance at all. No protests. No bothersome attempts to defend yourself or condemn me. If you expose your true circumstances, he'll become reckless."

Dinah dug her fingernails into the gallery railing and trained her gaze on a magnificent flowering tree across the courtyard. Its serene beauty was an ironic contrast that helped to focus her anguish.

"You gentlemen will be staying with us a few days," Valdivia called cheerfully. He stepped between Dinah and Sara, then put an arm around each of them. "I can't tell you how much it concerns me that you attempted to kidnap my beautiful ladies. They serve me well. I can't permit people to whisk them away, can I? So I must decide what to do with you."

Dinah started when Rucker's voice pierced her stoic facade. His deep, melodic drawl would have done justice to a master orator. He spent several seconds calmly giving Valdivia a lesson in colloquial southern obscenities.

"That about sums it up," Jeopard agreed.

Drake stood silent, but the murderous smile on his face and the slow flexing of his enormous hands spoke volumes. Valdivia applauded merrily then gave a command to the guards. They herded Rucker and the others out of the courtyard.

Dinah leaned against one of the gallery's columns and gazed at Valdivia with undisguised hatred. Sara turned numbly away. He bowed to them both.

"Smile, ladies. Tomorrow is National Founders' Day. The biggest holiday in Surador. Even rumors of revolution can't stop the festivities. It will be such fun."

"I'm going to hurt you somehow," Dinah told him.

Laughing and nodding, Valdivia strode away.

Rucker stood in the center of the small, square room that served as his cell and quietly told her to get out.

Dinah shook her head. She knew that she couldn't fight his anger or his distrust right now, but she could force him to accept the care he so badly needed.

She nodded to the small camera high in one corner of the room. "The guards are watching and listening. If you don't do what I tell you to do, they'll just come in and chain you to the bed. And *then* I'll do what I came to do."

He wanted to rage at her, she could tell. A muscle flexed in his jaw and his whole body was a study in resistance. She had seen the fierce, proud way he straightened his back when she came into the room, and she knew that he would never display either his physical or emotional pain.

"What did you come to do?" he asked grimly.

Dinah nodded toward the large wicker basket in her arms. "I have some liniment. And some food. Plus I brought you a comb and some clean clothes."

"Why?"

Because I love you, she wanted to say, but with the guards listening she could only mutter, "You're the father of my child. I owe you."

"Leave the stuff and get out. An alley cat has more loyalty to its mate than you do."

Dinah ignored his bitterness. "You have two choices, Rucker. Voluntary cooperation or forced cooperation. The former is much less humiliating."

He was seething, but trapped. Her heart went out to him in ways he could never know.

"What do you want me to do?" he demanded.

"Take your shirt off and lay down on the cot."

She winced as he whipped the green military T-shirt off his torso. The stiff movements of his arms announced his injuries despite his gallant effort to hide them. He stood before her, feet braced, chest moving rapidly, eyes full of anger. Dinah swept a cool gaze over the bruises on his torso and willed the pit of her stomach to relax.

She couldn't indulge her great need to take him in her arms and soothe every mark with a kiss.

"To the cot," she instructed. "I haven't got all day."

Lines of sarcasm bracketed his mouth. "Face up or face down?"

"Face up, please."

He stretched out, his booted feet hanging off the end of the bed, and put his hands behind his head. She noted that the past week's traumas had honed a few more pounds from his body.

The khaki fatigue pants gaped over the flat surface of his belly, which was terraced with muscle. His face was more angular than ever, and his untrimmed mustache had developed a dramatic droop on either side of his mouth. It made him look like some sort of handsome desperado from the wild west.

She gasped softly. He was a stranger—a tall, rangy package full of anger and pain, which was entirely directed toward her. She was afraid to touch him.

Dinah took several steadying breaths as she put her basket on a narrow tabletop. "You were very foolish today," she told him. "You can't beat Valdivia. You can only antagonize him."

"Is that what happened to Kyle Surprise? Did you help trap Kyle so Valdivia could turn a pack of rottweilers loose on him?"

Dinah busied herself getting liniment from her basket. The memory of Kyle's bravery would stay with her the rest of her life. He had been her and Sara's only hope, and he died because he tried to help them.

"No," she retorted. "I couldn't do something like that, no matter what you think. Don't ask me anymore. Ignorance is bliss, Rucker. And it's your only defense, as far as Valdivia is concerned."

Dinah went to the bed and knelt beside it. Rucker stared resolutely at the room's beamed ceiling. Tension radiated off him like heat on hot pavement. His broad chest rose and fell swiftly.

She cleared her throat anxiously. He looked as if he might explode with violence. Dinah covered her fingers with liniment and slid them over his bruised ribs. Her touch sent a quiver through them both. Dinah shut her eyes, and the fear left her senses as quickly as it had come. Memories flooded her mind.

"What is it?" she had asked. "An ear muff with legs?"

"A baby fox." He opened his cupped hands a bit and revealed a quivering little head with charcoal eyes. One of the fox's ears was torn and bleeding. "He was out behind the garage. I think a dog chewed him."

"I'll get some antiseptic and a washcloth. But I warn you—Jethro and Nureyev have trouble adjusting to your never-ending parade of furry patients. The raccoon drove them nuts. Are you going to keep the fox very long?"

"Till he's healed." He crooned ridiculous things to the tiny animal.

"You're a wonderful softy, Mr. McClure."

He frowned with grand dismay. "I'm tough as a board and twice as splintery."

She smiled. "Well, Wood Head, what are you going to name the fox?"

"Knothole . . . hey, hmmm, what did I do to deserve a kiss?"

No, there was nothing brutal in the soul of the man who trembled under her hands now and cursed his reaction.

"Sssh," she soothed. "I'm not trying to upset you."

"What did you drug me with at Anna Scarborough's?"

Dinah bowed her head. "I didn't drug you. Anna did it. I had no idea she was going to. I woke up beside you and was frightened when I realized what she'd done."

His large hands gripped the iron railing at the head of the bed. "But you walked out and left me laying there."

"Yes. I had to. Anna was supposed to tell you what happened."

She circled her fingers over his stomach for a moment then put more liniment on them and rubbed his chest again. The liniment's spicy eucalyptus scent filled her nose. "Lower your arms by your sides, please," she told him.

"Yes, of course. I want to be thoroughly relaxed when Valdivia sics the killer hounds on me."

Her chin snapped up. Dinah angrily rubbed liniment into the smooth hollows around his collar bones. "I'm doing my best to get you released."

"Oh?" His sardonic tone of voice made it clear that he didn't believe her. "What about Jeopard and Drake? I'm not goin' to leave them here."

"You talk as if you had choices."

He chuckled harshly. "We're like the Three Stooges, you know. I'm Larry, Jeopard's Mo, and Drake's the biggest damned Curly you've ever—"

"I'm doing what I can for them, too. But you're an American civilian. They're agents."

"What are you doing? Earnin' more sable coats?"

Her hand froze over his left nipple, where she had been distractedly caressing its brown nub. Almost of their own volition her fingers pinched him soundly.

Amazed, he turned his head and looked at her. "Is this some sort of torture? The 'Beauty Queen Finger-nail Technique' or something like that?"

Dinah looked at him miserably. "Why don't you just keep quiet and let me finish this?"

His mouth thinned. "You're finished." He started to sit up, and every inch of movement produced a corresponding expression of pain on his face.

Dinah flattened a hand over his navel and commanded, "Lay down or you'll be chained down."

Cursing, he sank back on the bed. She slid her fingers down his belly and just slightly under the waistband of his pants.

"Nobody hit me *there*."

Dinah tossed her head sardonically. "Too bad. I had other horrors in mind for below the waist." She moved her attention to his arms and began massaging the corded biceps. "Did Jeopard say anything about his being injured below the waist? From Sara Scarborough's well-aimed foot, I mean."

"Yeah. He said he was ready to sing soprano for a minute."

"Jeopard has a sense of humor. Amazing."

"And he loved his brother. The Iceman is very human, after all."

Silence descended. The skin of his arm was hot and smooth beneath her palm; his muscles felt like strips of hard rubber. She dabbed liniment onto her other hand and kneaded the thick cords on the tops of his shoulders.

They relaxed slowly. Dinah knew that her touch was a powerful weapon that diffused his anger. He shut his eyes and whispered wearily, "I hate this."

"Don't fight me. You're stuck here and you need my help. You've been beaten up, you're exhausted, you need to sleep. You can barely hold your eyes open now."

"Your concern is real suspicious." Despite his hard words, the rhythm of his chest began to slow. Dinah spent the next few minutes quietly stroking his arms from shoulder to wrist. Finally, he gave up.

She watched his facial muscles relax and her heart twisted at the vulnerability they revealed. Dinah bent over him and said softly, "I'll be back tonight, and I'll bring Katie."

Those words bridged the barrier of his defenses. He nodded groggily, and seconds later he was asleep.

Valdivia raised a heavy crystal goblet in salute. It caught the candlelight and scattered flecks of it over the lavish table settings. The shadowy room was a perfect backdrop for his black hair and midnight eyes. Dinah couldn't shake the feeling that darkness emanated from Valdivia like the outpouring of a sun in negative.

"To bargains, *querida*."

She raised her goblet and clinked it to his. "To honoring bargains." He sipped his wine and shook his head as if in self-rebuke.

Dinah's heartbeat began a thready patter. "It's time to be honorable, Diego," she insisted firmly. "You promised that we could leave when the project was finished. You have your herbicide. You've tested it, and you know that it works. Let Sara and Katie and me go. Let me take my husband and his companions with us. They were here on their own, not as representatives of the United States. Send them home. As long as you stay outside the U.S. they can't bother you."

The corners of his mouth turned down in teasing melancholy. "Oh, yes, they have much potential for causing me more trouble. And it would be so easy to make them disappear."

"Sara and I have cooperated with you all these months. Don't we deserve a favor?"

He clucked reproachfully. "You were forced to cooperate, remember?"

"But we could have made your mission much more difficult."

Valdivia sighed and leaned back in his chair. "I fear it's time to destroy your illusions, *querida*. I won't honor my bargain with you and Sara."

This was the moment Dinah had feared for ten months. Still, she was stunned. "All this time you let us think—"

"That I was honorable, yes. I am, but at a price. I'll make you one offer, a very good one, actually." He smiled. "An offer you can't refuse. Ah! I loved Señor Brando in that movie!"

His smile faded and he leaned forward. "The two agents must die. There's no other way. But they'll die painlessly, I promise you. Your husband and Sara can leave. I guarantee their safe trip back to the States." He paused. "You and Catalina must stay with me permanently."

Dinah gripped the table edge and fought the urge to sling one of the heavy candelabra at him. "And I'll be your mistress?"

"Yes."

It was sick, ludicrous, like a scene from an old movie. *Polly Purebred And El Diablo*, Dinah thought with a tinge of giddy hysteria. All Valdivia needed was a cape and a mustache to twirl.

"You can't be serious," she said.

"Do you want to watch your husband die?" He studied her face for a moment. "Obviously not. Good. I've been patient with you too long. I haven't had a woman since you arrived here. A noble sacrifice on my part, I'm sure you agree."

She rose slowly and walked to a window. The sun was sinking in brilliant golds and purples, casting magical light into the gardens below. Evening breezes brought her the poignant scents of flowers. She absorbed the nuances of the scene in a desperate attempt to fill the aching emptiness inside her chest.

If she submitted, Rucker would go home. She and Katie might eventually escape. If she didn't submit, Rucker would die.

She heard Diego rise and cross the room. He stopped beside her. "An answer, if you please."

Dinah turned toward him, inclined her head, and spoke bitterly. "I despise you. But I'll do what you want."

"*Bueno.* You'll spend the day with me tomorrow. Even with revolution brewing in Surador, the holiday will be glorious. Music, dancing, drinking—a daylong fiesta for everyone on the plantation. Now smile."

The fiesta. Dinah bit her lower lip to keep her face neutral as a dangerous idea began to take shape. Finally, she forced a thin semblance of a smile.

Valdivia spread his hands wide and laughed. "Am I not a gracious man?"

Rucker's gaze burned into her the moment she stepped into his room. He leaned against the wall near a window, away from the light of a small lamp beside his cot. He crossed his arms over his chest and remained immobile, a taunting and enigmatic force in the shadows.

As she had done during her first visit, Dinah nodded to the basket in her arms. But this time she said, "I told you that I'd bring Katie."

That reminder galvanized him. He came to her and held out his arms for the basket. Dinah looked up into his face and began memorizing every well-loved feature of it. Her throat knotted with grief.

She would never see him again after tomorrow. And if her plan worked, Katie would go with him, along with Sara, Jeopard, and Drake.

Dinah's arms seemed disconnected from her body. Finally she regained her concentration and handed the basket to him. She was glad that he was studying Katie.

His eyes were so beautiful, she thought as she watched his gaze soften. Katie's eyes had the same shade of green in them, but they held tinges of blue as well.

"Isn't she the most gorgeous baby you've ever seen?" Dinah whispered.

"Yes." Rucker went to his cot and sat down. Dinah walked to a chair by the window and lowered herself wearily. Everything she loved was about to be ripped away from her.

Seated in the shadows, she watched Rucker set the basket on the floor and lift Katie from it. The baby wore an embroidered pink top and diapers. He held her up and scrutinized her from head to toe.

"She came with all the correct parts," Dinah teased hoarsely.

"She's perfect."

Bittersweet happiness seeped into Dinah's despair. Katie and Rucker were going to be safe. It was more than she'd thought possible, and all she could hope for. No, not all—she prayed that Rucker would believe the truth when Sara finally had a chance to explain it to him.

"Does she talk yet?" he wanted to know.

"She's the child of a brilliant mother—of course she talks. Yesterday I caught her reciting the Gettysburg Address." Dinah smiled and shook her head when he shot a frown her way. "She's only three months old. She just makes noises."

As if on cue, Katie emitted a gurgling squawk. Rucker's eyes widened. "What was that, sweetpea? Lord, you sound like that cat in *Bloom County*. Yeah. Bill the Cat. *Ack.*"

Dinah warmed to the light-hearted mood Katie inspired. "Sometimes she does impressions. *Brrrrr,* like the big cicadas in the hacienda's garden. She tries to copy sounds."

He placed Katie on his knee and bounced her gently. Dinah suddenly noticed that he still wore his fatigue pants and khaki T-shirt. "Was something wrong with the clothes I brought you?"

"Yeah. I didn't want to look like a calypso singer." He paused. "White pedal pushers *ain't* the right pants for me. I like my pants to reach my ankles."

"They're not pedal pushers. Most of the men around here wear them."

"Valdivia's serfs wear them, you mean. No, thanks."

"Have I told you lately that you have more pride than a frog has tongue?"

"I taught you that sayin'. Don't use it against me." Katie waved her hands merrily and gurgled at him. "She's droolin'."

"Babies do that."

He peered at his daughter comically. "Did you inherit that from me? Well, little lady, I only drool when somebody offers me good barbecue. Now cut it out." He gently wiped her chin with the back of his index finger.

Dinah took a deep breath. Trying to keep her voice casual, she remarked, "She doesn't cry very often, and when she does she usually just needs to be fed or changed. She's accustomed to breast milk, but it won't be difficult to switch to a bottle."

It was important that he get this information. "She likes bright colors. And she likes to be talked to."

Fumbling, ignoring the curious look he was giving her, she went on. "Little girls should be encouraged to try the same things little boys try, don't you think? I mean, if Katie wants to play Little League baseball, I'd encourage her. Wouldn't you? And if she likes trains better than dolls, then you should—"

"Whoa," he interjected, his eyes fierce. "Why are you tellin' me this?"

Dinah was thankful for the shadows that hid her torment. "Well, if anything should happen to me, Katie would live with you."

He was suddenly very still. "What could happen to you?"

Dinah hugged her stomach as if in physical pain but made a pretense of speaking casually. "My goodness, Rucker, nothing. But if something *did*—"

"Like prison, when you finally get caught." His tone was icy.

She nodded. "Yes."

The tension was broken by Katie's soft, mewling cries. Dinah rose and went to Rucker's side. "Listen carefully," she told him. "That's a 'feed me' sound. If left ignored, it gets worse in a few minutes. *Much* worse."

"You don't have to leave, do you?"

Dinah stared down at him and caught the barely concealed regret in his eyes. Her legs went rubbery and she lowered herself beside him on the cot. "No. Not if you don't mind watching while I feed her."

His expression became a mask of controlled emotion. "I don't mind."

Dinah turned to face him, her back to the annoying camera on the wall. She unbuttoned the pearl gray blouse she wore with matching silk slacks. Her cheeks warmed a little as she unfastened one cup of her nursing bra. "Ugliest piece of underwear ever made," she muttered, lowering the material.

"Uh-huh," he agreed in a vague tone.

Dinah glanced up and found his eyes riveted to her exposed breast. She looked back down. The stiff bra support made it jut forward strangely. The nipple was a dark peak against a pale background laced with blue veins.

"It's not the most attractive sight at the moment," she said awkwardly. "In this contraption." When he continued to gaze at her with troubled eyes, she ventured, "What are you thinking?"

Resignation clouded his eyes, and his shoulders slumped a little. "Nothing about your body is ugly to me. I wish I didn't still feel that way about it, but I do."

"Oh, Rucker . . ."

"I was thinking about all the years we had together as lovers. And all the years we'll never have."

She dug her fingernails into her palms to keep from reaching for him.

"We were great together, Dee. I don't think you can deny that."

Was it possible to die inside and not show evidence of it? "I won't try to deny it. We're still great together."

He held up one hand, warning her to stop. "There's no point in puttin' on a show anymore. After you left me at Anna's I knew we were finished."

Dinah struggled for control. She didn't want to ruin their last night together with a useless effort to prove her sincerity.

"Rucker? If Katie turns out to be pretty—or beautiful —I hope she won't enter any beauty pageants."

He looked at her quizzically. "Why? I thought you enjoyed them."

"I did. But I also missed a lot of fun because I was always dieting and exercising and worrying about the next competition. Don't let Katie miss the fun of grow-ing up."

"Why do you keep talkin' as if you weren't gonna be around? There's not any guarantee that I'll get out of South America alive, much less take Katie away from you."

Dinah's throat convulsed for a moment. She swal-lowed hard. "Valdivia is letting you go home. After the holiday."

Rucker's astonishment kept him speechless for a mo-ment. Then, in a subdued tone, he asked, "But not Jeopard and Drake?"

"That's still undecided." She *couldn't* destroy the fragile mood by telling him what fate Valdivia intended for his companions. Besides, Jeopard and Drake would be free by tomorrow too, if her plan worked.

"Why just me?"

Because I bartered myself for your safety. Dinah searched for an acceptable answer, and felt the hair on the back of her neck rise with caution. The camera would pick up every word. "Because you don't know enough to do Valdivia any harm—which is exactly why I refused to tell you very much back in the States. And because he's protected here. You're an annoyance, not a threat. He has friends in the Suradoran government who would never allow him to be extradited just be-cause you made charges against him."

"What if there's a revolution and he loses his friends?"

"He'll have plenty of time to get out."

"And you? Will you go with him?"

Dinah felt as if Valdivia's hands were crawling up her back. Goose bumps broke out on her arms. "Of course."

"I thought your project was finished. That you were gonna leave him."

Dinah suppressed a bitter smile. "Plans change."

Rucker's gaze seethed with disgust. "What is it? Loy-alty? Some sort of ideals you have to follow? Money?"

If they didn't change the subject, she would break

into violent shivers. "All of the above," she lied. A full-fledged cry of hunger rose from Katie's mouth then, and Dinah sighed gratefully. "Here. Let me hold her."

He placed Katie in her arms then sat back, a strained expression on his face. "Was it hard for her to learn to nurse?" Rucker asked finally. "I mean, are human babies like puppies? Do they just nuzzle around until they find dinner and latch on?"

"Yes." Dinah frowned at her dry nipple.

"What's wrong?"

"Usually my milk comes down when Katie starts to cry. My body responds to her signal." She knew why the milk hadn't come; the stress of her grief and inner turmoil was affecting it.

Dinah cradled Katie to her breast and immediately the baby's little mouth sought it. After a few seconds of unsuccessful nursing, Katie's face contorted in tearful frustration.

Dinah's eyes burned. Even this basic act of sharing would be denied her during her last few hours with Rucker and their daughter. Turning her face away from him, she couldn't stop the tears that gathered on her eyelashes.

"What's wrong?" he asked again, his voice tortured.

"I can't nurse her."

"Because I'm watching?"

She shook her head. "I know you hate the idea of touching me, but could you rub my back? It might relax me."

Slowly, his jaw clenched, he nodded. Rucker moved around behind her and settled on the small bed. When his hands curled over her shoulders she quivered desperately. His fingers dug into her skin.

"Is it guilt or fear?" he demanded.

"I just wish that everything had worked out the way I wanted. I had hoped . . . hoped to come back to the States with Katie."

His hands rough, Rucker jerked her silk shirt down to her elbows. "Then why don't you?"

"Diego has requested that I stay."

"And what Diego wants, Diego gets. Well, he doesn't get Katie. I'll be back for her."

"Sssh!" Dinah frowned over her shoulder at him. "Nothing you say is private."

"I'll be back," Rucker emphasized. "And if Valdivia doesn't suspect that, he's a fool."

Her head drooped in defeat as his hands gripped her shoulders harshly. Katie burst into whimpers as she sensed the turmoil. Rucker's hold gentled.

"Let's just change the subject," he ordered.

Dinah nodded wearily. His fingertips began to caress her with languid, gentle motions. She felt the pressure of each coarse pad as he drew lines down the center of her back.

He put a hand on the crown of her head and stroked the length of her brunette hair. He ran both hands up the nape of her neck and spread her hair across her shoulders like a dark brown cape. Then he gathered it between her shoulder blades and smoothed it down her back before returning to his slow massage.

Several minutes passed before he stopped. "Does that help?" he murmured.

"Yes." Dinah watched Katie's face relax and felt the familiar warmth of milk seeping from her breast. "I knew your touch would make a difference. Thank you."

He pulled himself close to her and looked over her shoulder at the nursing baby. Dinah heard his soft inhalation of wonder. She felt his breath on her skin, smelled his earthy, arousing scent, and couldn't resist.

Turning her head, she brushed a kiss across his cheek. He shut his eyes, but didn't pull away. Slowly he tilted his head and gazed into her eyes. They shared a moment of poignant tenderness.

"We did one thing right, at least," he whispered in a ragged tone. "We made Katie. And we both love her. Whatever turned you away from me doesn't make any difference on that point."

Her voice was a mere breath of sound. "Nothing turned me away. I swear it. I can't go home with you, but I'll never stop loving you."

He shook his head, not believing her, but his anger seemed to be submerged in numb sorrow. He put his arms around her and kissed her temple then pressed his cheek to her hair.

"Would you do me a whimsical favor?" she asked in a voice drenched in tears. "Would you hum 'Amazing Grace'?"

After a moment of surprise he complied. Dinah shut her eyes and absorbed the low, throbbing music from his throat, so close beside her ear. She said all the prayers she needed to say then let her head tilt back against his shoulder.

He'd lulled her this way innumerable times in the past, and the memories brought her peace. Katie finished nursing and fell asleep, her small pink mouth relaxed against Dinah's breast.

Rucker put a hand on Katie's head. The other he slipped around Dinah's waist. "Tonight we're a family, and nothin' can change that," he whispered angrily. "Don't ever forget what you've given up."

"I won't." That was all the answer she could manage. Dinah stroked his hand as it cupped their daughter's delicate head. Now that her decisions were made and her future laid out, she was serene.

She would stay beside Valdivia during tomorrow's holiday revelry. By the time her plot was discovered, Rucker, Katie, Sara, Jeopard, and Drake would be safe.

She had no idea what Valdivia would do to her when he found out, but her victory would still be sweet.

Eleven

The rapid-fire tattoo of firecrackers woke Dinah shortly after dawn. She scooted out of bed as Katie began to protest loudly. Drawing a blue silk robe around a matching gown, Dinah went to an antique wicker bassinet and lifted Katie into her arms.

"Sssh, honey, they're just holiday noises." She crooned while walking to the barred window. Dinah gazed dully out. The pretty little village of the plantation workers lay beyond a line of trees in the distance. The popping firecrackers came from that direction.

Dinah turned her head toward the familiar rattle of the lock on the double doors to her suite. A lithe young woman entered the room bearing a silver tea service on a heavy silver tray.

"Good morning, Teodora."

Teodora nodded quickly. She was dressed in her feista clothes—a bright print skirt, a white blouse that exposed the tops of her shoulders, and delicate leather sandals.

But her anxious expression held no holiday spirit. "My compatriots are near the hacienda," she whispered, glancing around the room as if Valdivia might have hidden someone there. Teodora set the tray on a wicker cart that matched the rest of the room's Victorian furnishings. "Dr. Sara gave me the medicine to put in the guards' beer."

Katie had quieted. Dinah placed her back in the bassinet and went to a dressing table. She picked up a sealed letter and handed it to Teodora. The young Suradoran's eyes filled with tears.

"Bless you, Señora," she whispered.

Dinah grasped her shoulders. "You're very brave, and I'll never forget you. Give that letter to my husband, and he'll make certain that you reach your brother's home in Miami."

"Señora, isn't there some way you can come with us?"

Dinah shook her head. "This is the only day my plan will work. Everyone will be too busy enjoying the fiesta to notice what's happening. But Valdivia wants me beside him today. I have to be there to keep him distracted."

Dinah glanced toward Katie, and her throat tightened. "You'll come for her in a little while?"

"Yes. Don't worry, Señora, Dr. Sara and I will get her away." Teodora began to cry softly. "I feel so proud of you, Señora. I see how much you love your baby and your husband."

"Yes," Dinah murmured hoarsely.

Teodora hugged her. "I'll go now. You need this last time with your daughter."

Dinah's voice was hollow. "Yes."

After the doors closed behind Teodora, Dinah carried Katie to the bed and lay down with her. From around her own neck Dinah removed a short gold chain. On it were the wedding band and engagement ring she'd hidden from Valdivia's jealous eyes all these months. She fastened the chain around Katie's neck and stroked her cheek with a trembling finger.

Dee, our wedding bands'll be heirlooms, okay? My

family never had any traditions—unless you count Pa gettin' drunk every Saturday night. I want to start some.

She had nodded, pleased. Her family had thrived on tradition. "We can will the rings to our children, my darling. How about that?"

"Fine. Do you really like them? I'm not too good at pickin' nice things. You know that. The last time I shopped for a suit without your help, the salesman laughed at me. He said I must be color blind."

"I love the rings." She gestured at the gorgeous Acapulco scenery beyond the balcony of their honeymoon suite. "You picked this hotel. It's fantastic." Dinah touched the creamy white negligee she wore. "You picked this gown. It's perfect. I should find that salesman and wallop him for making fun of my boy."

Rucker slipped his arms around her. His eyes gleamed with amusement and pleasure. "Would you? I'd pay to see that."

She lifted her chin wryly. "Absolutely. As soon as we get back."

"It'll be like watchin' Princess Di mud wrestle."

Dinah smacked his bare chest in rebuke. "I know I'm too stuffy."

His hands roamed down her body. "The stuff of dreams." He smiled at the sloe-eyed look of delight she gave him. "Ladybug, you're not stuffy. Stuffy is made up of prejudice and selfishness and narrow-mindedness." His drawl deepened dramatically. "You ain't none of that. You're classy."

"And you're not?"

He smiled. "No more than stew meat compares to prime rib."

Dinah shook her head in reproach. She caught his mouth in a long, sweet kiss and circled her arms around his neck. "I've seen you make friends with people the rest of the world wanted to ignore," she whispered. "I've seen you be honest with people when nobody would know if you weren't. I've seen you show incredible patience to people who don't deserve it."

She paused, her eyes mischievous. "I've seen you throw pillows at the television when laxative commercials come on. Now *that's* a sign of class."

He chuckled with a warm, rich sound centered in deep happiness. "I have my standards."

She reached behind her back and grasped his left hand. Drawing that hand to her mouth, she kissed his wedding band. "Now you do mine." She held her hand up.

Rucker kissed her rings, nibbled her finger, and winked. "I sealed them on. You're a marked woman." He carried her to bed.

Dinah laughed. "I like your traditions."

She had hoped to help him start so many others.

Dinah blinked back her reverie and with it her tears. Valdivia must not suspect that her emotions were a shambles. She brushed her lips across Katie's forehead.

"Take care of your father for me, my darling," Dinah whispered brokenly. "And love him as much as I do."

Rucker paced in his sweltering room, listening to the distant sounds of music, firecrackers, and boisterous gunfire. He'd endured the celebration all day, and it had worn on his nerves because he kept wondering whether Dinah was celebrating with Valdivia.

The door to his room jerked open. A swarthy young man in peasant clothing stood there. An automatic rifle hung casually in his hands. Jeopard and Drake stood behind him.

"Don't ask questions," Jeopard instructed. "Just get out of there."

Rucker followed them down a wide hallway decorated with colorful rugs and pre-Colombian artifacts. He stared at several armed men who lay sprawled unconscious on the floor, empty mugs beside them. "What the hell?"

Jeopard glanced over one shoulder. "Sara Scarborough has her mother's talent."

Rucker frowned. Why would Sara help them escape? Their guide led them through a maze of hallways and down a set of steps into a dank, underworld area stocked with wine bottles and rats. He swung a narrow wooden door open and grinned at them.

"Freedom," he said with a heavy Spanish accent.

"Whoa," Rucker exclaimed softly. Jeopard and Drake eyed him. "Sara did this for us? Why?"

"No talk. Hurry. I like Americans," the guide said. He thumped his chest proudly. "Rebel. Ya-hoo. Same side. Clint Eastwood."

Rucker knew he ought to be relieved, but he felt as if his soul were being torn apart. He was leaving Dee. He directed his confused torment toward Jeopard. "So you're just gonna walk away? Valdivia killed your brother."

Jeopard retrieved a small glass vial from his shirt's breast pocket. It was half-full of amber liquid. "This is the prototype for the herbicide, courtesy of Sara. As soon as I get it to a safe place, I'll be back for Valdivia."

Rucker turned and looked in the direction from which they'd come, his breathing short, his heart pounding.

"Forget her," Jeopard ordered. "Sara thought things over and decided to help us. Apparently Dinah had the same chance and didn't take it."

Rucker swung back toward the open door, his thoughts surging with self-rebuke and bitterness. How could he still let himself be stupid enough to hope and to love?

He gestured fiercely. "Let's get out of here."

Night drew a romantic cover over the festivities. Glowing torches and lanterns highlighted tables heavy with food. The people who weren't too drunk to dance were whirling to the vibrant Latin rhythms of a loud band.

Valdivia wore white slacks with a loose white shirt.

Dinah moved woodenly through the crowd with her hand tucked in the crook of Valdivia's elbow. At his request, she wore a flowing white dress with multicolored embroidery around the scooped neck and short sleeves. His people made a pathway for them as if they were royalty.

Valdivia bent to whisper in her ear, "You see how wonderful life will be for you."

"Yes." She smiled and let him think she was content. In a way she was. Rucker and Katie were far away by now. Sara, Jeopard, and Drake were safe also.

"Patron!" One of Valdivia's aides pushed his way toward them. The man's eyes darted to Dinah, then settled fearfully on Valdivia. "The Americans are gone. All. Including Dr. Scarborough."

Dinah felt a muscle convulse in Valdivia's arm. When he turned to look at her, his gaze was murderous. Her smile widened.

The last thing Rucker expected to see when they reached the rebel camp was his daughter in the arms of Sara Scarborough. A young Suradoran woman stood beside them. Both women looked exhausted, and both appeared on the verge of emotional collapse.

Stunned, Rucker stopped in front of them and stared down at Katie. She stirred restlessly in Sara's arms and looked at him with unhappy blue-green eyes. His gaze flickered to the necklace she wore.

A hard fist twisted in Rucker's stomach. There was something horribly wrong. Dinah would never give up Katie or her wedding rings. He struggled for an explanation that would appease his cynicism.

"She doesn't want our baby any more?" he asked Sara.

"Oh. Oh, stop!" Those words seemed to be all she could manage.

"I'm tired of not gettin' any answers." Rucker took

Katie from Sara's arms. He realized that Jeopard and Drake were staring at the scene in quiet curiosity. He realized that he was trembling all over.

"Why did Dinah send Katie to me?" he asked in a low, fierce voice.

Sara straightened and cleared her throat. Rucker gritted his teeth in frustration at the evidence of her careful deception.

Sara shrugged elaborately. "She doesn't want Katie involved in her work."

"Tell me the truth."

"Valdivia doesn't like children."

He bit the words harshly. "Tell me the truth."

Sara shook her fists at him. "Dammit, McClure, Dinah wants you to take Katie and go home! I gave her my word that you'd do that! Get that through your thick skull and quit interrogating me!"

"She doesn't love me anymore, but she loves Katie dearly. There's no way in hell she'd give her up."

"Well she did, and you should honor her decision and *go home*."

Rucker's voice rose to a shout. "Tell me the truth!"

"I told you the . . ."

"Sweet angels forgive me, I can't keep my word!" The woman beside Sara fell to her knees and grasped Rucker's legs. Sobbing, she looked up at him.

"Señor, your wife is the one who planned the escape for everyone. She is the bravest woman I've ever known. Everything she does, she does to help you and the others. She does it for love of you and the baby."

"Teodora, be quiet!" Sara cried. "This isn't what Dinah wanted!"

Teodora shook her head wildly. "And she knows that Valdivia will kill her for doing it! Save her!"

Dinah heard soft, scurrying sounds in the darkness. Water dripped from somewhere above, trailing down the side of her face. The ground was wet underneath her, and the air smelled stale. Her feet bound, her eyes blindfolded, her hands tied behind her, she huddled against the unknown. She couldn't stop shivering.

Think small, she told herself. *Think invisible.*

Valdivia's last words echoed in her mind. "This is just the beginning, *querida.* Enjoy the company down here tonight. It will be the most pleasant company you will have for a long, long time."

If she concentrated on the night ahead, she'd panic. So instead she sorted through her memories.

I was not meant to traipse through slimy tunnels in the dark, Rucker.

"It's called spelunking, ladybug. Stick close to me."

"Of course. You have the flashlight. You're the only living thing I trust down here."

"If you keep grabbin' my butt you won't even be able to trust me."

"Sir, I'm not 'grabbin' your butt.' I'm clutching your back pockets. Desperately."

"Here we are. Look. This is the cavern I told you about."

"Hmmm. Oh, Rucker! Oh, my."

"Look there. See how the walls glow when the light hits 'em? Phosphorescence. Minerals from millions of little fossilized sea critters. It's like a cathedral underground. Ahhh. A streak of purple. Gold. Every color. I think a rainbow got trapped in here. In the middle of all this darkness, the beauty still shines. It's you and me and a million years of magic. Babe? Babe, are you listenin'?"

"I could learn to like slimy places."

"Your voice sounds funny. You okay?"

"I'm crying."

"Dee? Do you want to leave?"

"No. You've given me something I'll never forget. Can't a girl cry over your poetry? What are . . . you're laughing at me."

"No, babe. But me a poet? I can't even think up a rhyme."

Oh, Rucker, if only this damned cellar had your rainbow in it.

The cellar shook. Dinah jerked awake from a strained sleep and cried out in confusion. A booming sound drowned out her voice, and vibrations showered her with bits of dirt and wood.

Were they having an earthquake? The terror of being helpless and trapped underground made her writhe desperately against her bonds.

But then she heard other sounds; staccato popping noises, the thud of running feet overhead, men shouting, and other garbled noises that signaled violence.

Revolution, she decided breathlessly. What if the rebels took over and there was no one left to tell them that she was a captive down here?

Her nerves screamed from the tension. The blood rushed against her eardrums so forcefully that she had trouble hearing. Dinah made herself take slow breaths and listen to the continuing sounds of battle upstairs.

Then she heard the dull groan of the cellar's heavy double doors opening. A single pair of feet hurried down a flight of stone stairs.

Dinah's mouth went dry as the footsteps came toward her across the uneven stone floor. The sharp brightness of a flashlight invaded her blindfold. A hand wound into her hair.

"We're going to put on a little show, *querida,*" Valdivia told her pleasantly. "It will be my finale, I'm afraid. But I'll enjoy it."

She had no time to ask questions. The commotion upstairs birthed only one identifiable sound—that of another man coming down the cellar steps and then across the floor.

"Careful, Señor," Valdivia called. "Drop your gun or I'll shoot her."

The footsteps halted. There was a deadly pause, followed by the sound of a heavy weapon being placed on the floor. And then a dear voice shook Dinah to the core.

"If you hurt her, I'll make sure you die slow."

"Rucker," Dinah exclaimed softly, all her love in the name.

"Sit tight, ladybug."

"I will. Be careful."

Rucker's tone was low and deceptively casual. "You're done for, Valdivia. Killin' your own agent won't change anything."

Valdivia laughed softly. "Killing my own agent, Señor? But Dinah has never been my agent." His voice rang with malicious pride. "Do you know how I acquired your wife, Señor? *I stole her from you.*"

"I don't care how you convinced her to work for you. She's changed her mind. Let her go."

Valdivia's voice was suddenly somber. "You still don't understand. Amazing. You think she came to me of her own free will, yet you risk your life to save her? I salute your love for her. I envy her love for you. Yes, your wife loves you, Señor."

Dinah felt his hand loosen in her hair. She tilted her head back as if she were looking up at him. "Diego, nothing you do will change that."

Valdivia stroked her hair for an instant, then let his hand trail away. "I learned that long ago, *querida*," he said wearily. Then his tone became cheerful again. "Señor! Understand the truth! I kidnapped your wife! Now I give her back!"

More footsteps. A new voice spoke. "Get her out of here, Rucker. This bastard has called for government soldiers. He's stalling for time."

"Ah, Señor Surprise. How appropriate."

"Jeopard, I can't leave you here alone," Rucker interjected. "This is my fight, too."

"You've got Dinah back. I'll never get my brother back. Valdivia and I have to settle that. Go."

Dinah heard Rucker's footsteps come to her and stop. Then his hands were under her elbows, raising her up. With her feet bound, she tottered. He lifted her into his arms. She rested her head against his shoulder and gloried in the scent and feel of him.

"Good-bye, *querida*," Valdivia murmured. "May we meet again."

"God help you," she answered.

"Burn in hell," Rucker told him.

Dinah burrowed her face into Rucker's neck and rubbed off the blindfold as he carried her upstairs. She glanced back. The last thing she saw was Jeopard setting a lantern on the floor between himself and Valdivia.

Rucker kicked the cellar doors shut. He walked down a long hallway and out into one of the hacienda's courtyards. A full moon shone overhead.

He set her down carefully and knelt by her feet, his big hands fumbling with the nylon rope that bound her ankles. When they were free he stood and gently untied her hands. Then he simply stood still, gazing down at her in the golden moonlight.

"When you disappeared in Florida—you'd been kidnapped by Valdivia?" he asked.

She nodded and rose on tiptoe to kiss his tears.

The small band of rebels, worried about an attack by Suradoran soldiers, whisked Dinah and Rucker out of the hacienda. Rucker motioned to them to stop. "Tell them we can't leave Jeopard," he instructed Dinah.

She spoke to them in Spanish. Their leader answered. Dinah nodded. "They've stationed two men by the cellar doors to wait for him."

There was no more time for talk after that. The rebels led them in darkness and silence along narrow paths in the rain forest. Dinah's white dress was already a dirty, clinging mess from the hours she'd spent in the cellar; Rucker helped her rip a two-foot width of material from the bottom of the full skirt.

She was barefoot, so a rather large woman with the group offered a spare pair of brogans from her backpack. Dinah stuffed torn dress material into the toes to make them fit. Clumping along beside Rucker with her ragged skirt flapping around her thighs, Dinah imagined him grinning.

"Stop it," she whispered, and punched his arm.

The faint sound of his chuckle confirmed her suspicions.

Three hours later they reached the rebel camp. Drake Lancaster, who'd stayed behind with the herbicide, rose from a group of people seated around a fire and came toward them, his expression troubled as he searched for Jeopard.

Rucker briefly explained what Jeopard had done to avenge his brother's death. Drake shook his head and cursed softly. "I wish he'd known. Kyle's alive."

Stunned, Dinah stared at him speechlessly. Finally she managed, "No, he can't be. Sara and I were forced to watch. And when the dogs finished . . . and Valdivia's men dragged him away . . . it was terrible. Valdivia said he was dead."

"He wasn't, and Valdivia knew it. He sent Kyle to one of his other plantations and held him prisoner. The rebels just brought word that he escaped about a week ago. He's with them in the mountains. We've sent for him."

Dinah turned excitedly toward Rucker and grasped his hands. "Kyle knows the truth. He knows everything that Valdivia did to make Sara and Anna and me work for him. He can testify for us."

"Thank God," Rucker said gruffly. "But I still don't

know how any of this happened." His hands tightened around hers. Their eyes held, and Valdivia's revelation hung in the air as if he had just spoken it. "*Kidnapped*," Rucker repeated, his gaze dark.

Dinah rested her head against his shoulder. "Yes. Sara, too."

Sara and Teodora came out of a small tent and ran up to them, squinting in the light of camp fires and lanterns. They grabbed Dinah and hugged her.

Sara turned toward Rucker. "Stubborn man," she muttered. Then she threw her arms around him. One second after she let go, Teodora took her place.

"Bless you, Señor. Bless you."

Dinah touched Sara's arm anxiously. "Katie?"

"Asleep in the tent. She's fine."

A pained, bitter look came over Sara's face. "What happened to Valdivia?"

Dinah told her about him and Jeopard. "All we can do is wait."

The biologist nodded, her gaze distracted as if she were seeing the hell of the past months. "Valdivia isn't human. He can't be killed. Poor Jeopard."

"Sara? Rucker knows that we were kidnapped."

Sara nodded, her thoughts still dazed. In a low, vague tone she said, "I can't believe it's over. It's not real." Teodora patted her arm sympathetically, then guided her toward the fire.

The young Suradoran woman spoke over her shoulder to Rucker and Dinah. "Come. We'll get you food and something to drink."

Dinah looked up at Rucker and found that his gaze was already on her. They shared a tender look that shut out the rest of the world.

"Let's go see Katie first," he said gruffly.

Dinah slipped her hand through his and they walked to the small, dome-shaped tent. Inside it was dark and cool. A screened opening overhead outlined a patch of stars and the first traces of dawn.

Katie lay on her stomach atop a folded blanket. She was asleep, but when Dinah knelt and stroked her hair with a finger, she yawned.

Rucker curved one arm out in a beckoning gesture to Dinah. She nestled into the crook of it and they sat down. He was filthy and sweat stained. When he rested his jaw against her forehead his beard stubble scrubbed her skin. She didn't mind a bit.

Dinah smiled joyfully and pressed so close to him that she felt the rhythm of his heart against her own rib cage. They sat in silence for several minutes, just watching Katie sleep.

"I agree with Sara. None of this seems real," Dinah whispered. "What made you decide to come back for me?"

"Teodora broke down and told me that you planned everybody's escape, and that Valdivia would kill you because of it."

"But you still thought I was working for him?"

Rucker's voice was a low rumble. "Didn't matter anymore. You are the woman I love." He paused, and she felt his chest move harshly. "Why wouldn't you tell me the real story to begin with?"

Dinah slid a hand across the soft material of his khaki T-shirt and stroked the area over his heart. "Because you'd have stopped at nothing to help me and Katie. Even when you thought the worst, you were willing to take risks for me. I can imagine what you'd have done if you'd known the truth."

Dinah cleared her throat roughly. "Valdivia knew that the real story would create an international incident if it ever got out. A Russian agent sneaks into a U.S. resort town and kidnaps two innocent American civilians. Not exactly a plus for *glasnost*, hmmm? Valdivia's superiors would have had to sacrifice him if his activities were discovered."

Dinah shuddered. "So he made it very clear to me what kind of revenge he'd take if I ever told. When he found out that I was pregnant, he knew he had all the leverage he needed to make me do whatever he wanted. I saw how he hurt Kyle Surprise. Valdivia was capable of doing inhuman things to Katie and you. I couldn't take that chance, no matter how much I wanted to tell you the truth."

Rucker held her tighter. His voice ragged, he whispered. "There isn't a word good enough to describe your kind of courage. Dear lord, I was so bad to you. I nearly died when you disappeared, and when I thought that you'd run off with Valdivia, I wanted to hate you. I was so bad to you," he repeated.

"Sssh. You were reacting reasonably, under the circumstances. I knew that. It only hurt me because you were suffering and I desperately wanted to make things right again." He shivered with emotion. She caressed his face tenderly. "My darling, everything you've done over the past week and a half has only made me love you more."

She tilted her head back. Silent understanding brought him to her for a lingering kiss. His breath was soft against her mouth. "I'm gonna be overprotective of you and Katie. You'd better get used to the idea, 'cause I'll probably be a pain in the butt."

"I'm going to have trouble letting you out of my sight. You'd better get used to *that*, sir."

"Ain't no place I wanna go without you, ma'am."

She put her head back on his shoulder and they held each other possessively.

"Dee?"

"Hmmm?"

"There's still one thing I don't understand."

She could practically read his mind. "How I became involved with Sara and Anna's work."

"Yeah."

"They were trying to create a herbicide, but not the kind Valdivia wanted. Sara has done research in Surador for years. She discovered a plant-killing virus carried by certain species of butterflies, and she decided that it had potential as a mild, natural weed killer for agricultural use.

"I told you that I met Valdivia at the Conference of the Americas, two years ago. That's true. We talked casually and he said that he knew of Sara Scarborough's work. He was charming—and he didn't hide the fact that he was interested in me. I politely refused an invitation to spend the night with him and that was the end of it."

"Or so you thought," Rucker interjected. "That aggressive s.o.b."

Dinah nodded. "Anna started telling me about this Suradoran businessman named Valdivia who wanted to sponsor Sara's research. Sara was pleased until she learned that he was using his government connections to intercept mail from her mother. That made her mad and scared her. She told him to bug off—pardon the pun."

"But what did that have to do with you?"

"Anna wanted to send Sara some important notes and some butterfly cocoons, but she was afraid Valdivia would interfere again. When she heard that you and I were going to Florida on vacation, she arranged for Sara to meet me there."

Dinah raised her hands in supplication. "I was just supposed to give Sara the package. Butterfly cocoons. How simple." Her voice became sheepish. "I didn't tell you because the intrigue seemed so silly that I was embarrassed."

Rucker exhaled slowly, letting months of questions and anxiety evaporate into the night air. "So Valdivia ambushed you and Sara in Key West?"

"Yes. I was driving Sara back to her hotel. A half-dozen men in two vans forced me off the road. Valdivia was waiting in a separate car. When he saw me, he smiled and said, 'An unexpected treasure.' He was convinced that Sara and Anna's herbicide could be altered for military use. He took Sara hostage to force Anna's cooperation with the research."

Rucker's voice was pensive. "He put the two of you on a boat that night."

Dinah looked at him askance. "To Cuba. Yes. How did you know?"

"After the police called and told me that they'd found the car deserted on a back road, I sort of sleepwalked out of the beach house. I really didn't know what I was doin', but all of a sudden I was lookin' at the ocean. I felt that you were out there."

She cupped his face between her hands. "Did you know that all I was thinking about was you? I knew that you were going through hell."

He turned his head and kissed her palm. "It's nothin' compared to what you survived."

Dinah kissed him again. "The important thing is that we *both* survived. We love each other more than ever. We can go home. Oh, dear God, I want to go home so badly. And we have Katie."

Rucker chuckled hoarsely. "And Jethro. We still have our possum."

She laughed with delight. "We do?"

Rucker stroked her hair tenderly and nodded. "Nureyev got sick and died, babe. I did everything I could for him, but it was hopeless. Jethro's fat and happy, though. He's on loan to a petting zoo."

"The first thing we have to do when we get back is retrieve our possum."

Rucker smiled. "I like your priorities."

Drake's calm voice came to them from outside the tent. "Sorry to interrupt, but Jeopard's here."

Rucker and Dinah hurried to meet him. He stood by a camp fire with Sara and Teodora, his hands in the pockets of his khaki trousers, his face tired but relaxed.

He gazed somberly at Dinah, then at Sara, then back at the fire. "We talked a long time. He knew that his operation was blown. The Russians would disown him as soon as we put some pressure on them. They couldn't afford not to. He'd be an embarrassment to international relations. He told me how he kidnapped and coerced you two. He admitted that Kyle was alive. He said he only regretted one thing."

Jeopard glanced at Rucker, then Dinah. His eyes held hers, and it was clear that he thought Valdivia's last words were best left unsaid.

"I think we know," Rucker told him.

Dinah grasped her husband's hand and looked at Jeopard grimly. "What else happened?"

Jeopard's pause was intense. "He shot himself."

Dinah gasped and Rucker's arm slid around her. But she felt no horror or sadness. When she looked at Sara, Sara's eyes held quiet satisfaction. "Now we're really free," Sara said softly.

Dinah nodded in agreement.

Epilogue

She empathized with Dorothy in *The Wizard of Oz*. There was no place like home.

Her handsome, mustached wizard was stretched out on the couch wearing only gray sweatpants and reading the weekend edition of the Mount Pleasant newspaper. His rather large, bare feet were nestled in her lap, and he made happy sounds from time to time because she was massaging them.

A piano concerto floated from the tape deck sitting on a bookcase. The wine she'd had with dinner made her body feel deliciously languid; the soft caress of her filmy white nightgown helped.

Her munchkin queen was safe, happy, and asleep in the new nursery down the hall. Toto, in the form of a fat gray possum, was perched on the hearth. He stared impassively into a crackling pine-log fire and nibbled from a bowl of dry cat food.

Getting back to Kansas had taken considerably more effort than just tapping her heels together. She and Rucker had traveled from Surador to a special government facility in Virginia, where they went through a week of debriefing and medical tests.

But that wasn't a hardship; they had a nice suite of

rooms with a crib for Katie. They had plenty of time to play with her, to sleep off the physical exhaustion from their ordeal, to make love and care for each other in tender, intimate ways.

Sara stayed at the facility too, along with Anna. And Kyle.

Dinah frowned pensively, thinking of the terrible scars on his face and body, scars that no amount of plastic surgery could completely repair. He'd never been the kind of breathtakingly handsome man that Jeopard was, but he had been so charming and cheerful that women adored him anyway.

Kyle wasn't vain, but she could tell that the scars bothered him. She knew that he'd be all right in time, but for now he was restless and depressed. The Suradoran assignment seemed to have affected Jeopard in a similar way. She suspected that both men were brooding over their careers and lifestyles.

"Oh, no," Rucker groaned. "She printed it."

Dinah gazed at him curiously. The newspaper hid his face, but the quivering of his bare stomach gave away his silent laughter.

"What?" she asked warily.

"The reporter was new, but I thought she could tell that I was only joking—"

"Rucker, people are just beginning to get over the shock of having me back here. I hope you didn't stir things up again."

"Well," he said in a strangled tone.

"Rucker! We worked so hard on our cover story!"

"Sssh. This article is too ridiculous to make anybody ask questions."

Because the Suradoran incident had to remain classified, part of their debriefing time had been spent with a staff of agents who helped them concoct an explanation for the past ten months.

She'd been kidnapped by an extremist political group determined to gain a pardon for their leader, who was serving time in an Alabama prison. They'd hidden her in Canada, treated her well, and finally released her and her new daughter.

What mischief had Rucker done?

"I'm sorry, ladybug," he said, his voice strained with controlled mirth. "I'll call Lois Lane tomorrow and ask her to print a retraction."

Dinah twisted one of his toes. He yelped. "Read it out loud," she said fiendishly, "or this little piggy will never go to market again."

He cleared his throat in mock embarrassment and began. " 'Former Mayor Dinah McClure has returned to everyday activities after the sensational events of the past ten months, according to her husband, well-known writer Rucker McClure. McClure was interviewed last week following a speech to the Mount Pleasant Young Women's Luncheon Club.

" 'He said the story of her kidnapping was actually a polite cover-up. McClure insisted that his wife wandered for months after suffering amnesia. He said that she fell and struck her head while shooting craps with a shrimp boat crew during a vacation in Florida last summer.

" 'She'd gone to have her hair done,' McClure noted. 'But the shrimp boat dock was right next door. She never could resist a good game of craps. And she loves the smell of shrimp.' "

Dinah sank her head in her hands and moaned dramatically. "Is there more?"

"Uh, yes. But it's not important . . ."

"Read it, buster."

" 'McClure said that she returned to her car after the accident and drove away aimlessly. While he spent months searching for her, she worked her way north doing odd jobs. When investigators located her last month in Canada, she had adopted the name Lurleen Studebaker and was touring with a professional wrestling organization.' "

"Rucker, we're going to move to Tibet. Tomorrow. It's the only place I won't feel embarrassed."

" 'McClure said that his wife, a former beauty queen, didn't lose all recollection of her identity. While wrestling she billed herself as Miss Congeniality.' "

He put the paper down and gazed at her contritely. "That's all, Dee." His mouth was a tight line of restrained humor. "I'm real sorry."

"Sir, you haven't *begun* to be sorry."

His feet lay on a small throw pillow. She jerked it from under them, shoved his feet off her lap, and pounced on him, flailing him vigorously.

He laughed so hard that he could barely protect himself. Ducking, his arms raised, he rolled off the couch. She followed, whacking him across the back. He ran, holding his stomach with one hand. She chased.

They ended up in the bedroom. He dropped to his knees, cowered dramatically, and wiped tears of amusement from his eyes. She stood over him, the pillow drawn back with menace.

"I'll do anything to make up for it," he begged.

She scrutinized him for a moment, then flipped the switch on a nearby lamp and pointed to the bed. "Anything?"

He clutched his heart. "Even that."

What started as a boisterous romp gradually became a quiet sharing of pleasure. He made good on his apology, using his hands and mouth to convey all manner of regrets until she couldn't think clearly enough to remember what he was apologizing for.

Then he cradled her in his arms and slipped inside her, his body strong and sure, his mouth incredibly tender on her face and lips.

"Apology accepted?" he whispered when she lay smiling and limp under him.

"Hmmm." She reached for the pillow and weakly flapped it against his shoulder one last time. "Monster."

He lay down beside her and stroked her glistening

body. She fell asleep with his mouth and mustache tickling her ear.

When Dinah awoke she was alone. But he had covered her with a quilt, and she could hear him typing at his word processor in the next room.

Dinah put a robe on and crossed the hall to the nursery. Katie stirred lazily. "Let's go see what Daddy's up to now," Dinah whispered.

With Katie in her arms, she went to the office. Rucker sat there in his sweatpants, his aviator glasses perched on his nose, his brow furrowed in concentration.

"You're writing," she said in amazement.

He looked up and smiled. "It's time I got back to it." His eyes roamed over her and Katie. "What a pretty sight," he said softly. He pulled an old ottoman beside his office chair and patted it invitingly. "Sit a while and help me think."

She settled beside him and looked at the computer screen. "What do you have in mind?"

"A novel. Not a collection of anecdotes and stories like I've always done before. Serious fiction." He caressed Katie's cheek for a moment, then brushed his fingertips across Dinah's lips.

His eyes glowed with affection and contentment. "What do you think of that? Me bein' a serious writer?"

"I've always known you could do it."

"With you goin' back to school to get your doctorate, I need to work at home and help take care of Katie. Now's the perfect time to try a novel."

"Do you have an idea for a story?"

He nodded. "Us. What happened to us this year. I'll change the basics so much that nobody who knows the real story will make the connection. But the important things will be true." Rucker laid a hand along her cheek and studied her carefully. "Do you mind if I write about what happened? I'll need your help with it."

Her eyes gleamed with devotion. "I don't mind. I think it'll do us both good." Dinah hesitated then tilted her head quizzically. "What are 'the important things' you won't alter?"

For a moment he gazed at her and their daughter in silent reverence. Then he said softly, "The love. The faith."

She smiled an enduring *Yes*.

THE EDITOR'S CORNER

With the very special holiday for romance lovers on the horizon, we're giving you a bouquet of half a dozen long-stemmed LOVESWEPTs next month. And we hope you'll think each of these "roses" is a perfect one of its kind.

We start with the romance of a pure white rose, **IT TAKES A THIEF,** LOVESWEPT #312, by Kay Hooper. As dreamily romantic as the old South in antebellum days, yet with all the panache of a modern-day romantic adventure film, Kay's love story is a delight . . . and yet another in her series that we've informally dubbed "Hagen Strikes Again!" Hero Dane Prescott is as enigmatic as he is handsome. A professional gambler, he would be perfectly at home on a riverboat plying the Mississippi a hundred years ago. But he is very much a man of today. And he has a vital secret . . . one he has shouldered for over a decade. Heroine Jennifer Chantry is a woman with a cause—to regain her family home, Belle Retour, lost by her father in a poker game. When these two meet, even the sultry southern air sizzles. You'll get reacquainted, too, in this story with some of the characters you've met before who revolve around that paunchy devil, Hagen—and you'll learn an intriguing thing or two about him. This fabulous story will also be published in hardcover, so be sure to ask your bookseller to reserve a collector's copy for you.

With the haunting sweetness and excitement of a blush-pink rose, **MS. FORTUNE'S MAN,** LOVESWEPT #313, by Barbara Boswell sweeps you into an emotion-packed universe. Nicole Fortune bounds into world-famous photographer Drake Austin's office and demands money for the support of his child. Drake is a rich and virile heartbreaker who is immediately stopped in his tracks by the breathtaking beauty and warmth of Nicole. The baby isn't his—and soon Nicole knows it—but he's not about to let the girl of his dreams get out of sight. That means he has

(continued)

to get involved with Nicole's eccentric family. Then the fun and the passion really begin. We think you'll find this romance a true charmer.

As dramatic as the symbol of passion, the red-red rose, **WILD HONEY,** LOVESWEPT #314, by Suzanne Forster will leave you breathless. Marc Renaud, a talented, dark, brooding film director, proves utterly irresistible to Sasha McCleod. And she proves equally irresistible to Marc, who knows he shouldn't let himself touch her. But they cannot deny what's between them, and, together, they create a fire storm of passion. Marc harbors a secret anguish; Sasha senses it, and it sears her soul, for she knows it prevents them from fully realizing their love for each other. With this romance of fierce, primitive, yet often tender emotion, we welcome Suzanne as a LOVESWEPT author and look forward to many more of her thrilling stories.

Vivid pink is the color of the rose Tami Hoag gives us in **MISMATCH,** LOVESWEPT #315. When volatile Bronwynn Prescott Pierson leaves her disloyal groom at the altar, she heads straight for Vermont and the dilapidated Victorian house that had meant a loving home to her in her childhood. The neighbor who finds her in distress just happens to be the most devastatingly handsome hunk of the decade, Wade Grayson. He's determined to protect her; she's determined to free him from his preoccupation with working night and day. Together they are enchanting . . . then her "ex" shows up, followed by a pack of news hounds, and all heck breaks loose. As always, Tami gives us a whimsical, memorable romance full of humor and stormy passion.

Sparkling like a dew-covered yellow rose, **DIAMOND IN THE ROUGH,** LOVESWEPT #316, is full of the romantic comedy typical of Doris Parmett's stories. When Detective Dan Murdoch pushes his way into Millie Gordon's car and claims she's crashed his stakeout, she knows she's in trouble with the law . . . or, rather, the

(continued)

lawman! Dan's just too virile, too attractive for his own good. When she's finally ready to admit that it's love she feels, Dan gets last-minute cold feet. Yet Millie insists he's a true hero and writes a book about him to prove it. In a surprising and thrilling climax, the lady gets her man . . . and you won't soon forget how she does it.

As delicate and exquisite as the quaint Talisman rose is Joan Elliott Pickart's contribution to your Valentine's Day reading pleasure. **RIDDLES AND RHYMES**, LOVE-SWEPT #317, gives us the return of wonderful Finn O'Casey and gives him a love story fit for his daring family. Finn discovers Liberty Shaw in the stacks of his favorite old bookstore . . . and he loses his heart in an instant. She is his potent fantasy come to life, and he can't believe his luck in finding her in one of his special haunts. But he is shocked to learn that the outrageous and loveable older woman who owned the bookstore has died, that Liberty is her niece, and that there is a mystery that puts his new lady in danger. In midsummer nights of sheer ecstasy Liberty and Finn find love . . . and danger. A rich and funny and exciting love story from Joan.

Have a wonderful holiday with your LOVESWEPT bouquet.

And do remember to drop us a line. We always enjoy hearing from you.

With every good wish,

Carolyn Nichols

Carolyn Nichols
Editor
LOVESWEPT
Bantam Books
666 Fifth Avenue
New York, NY 10103